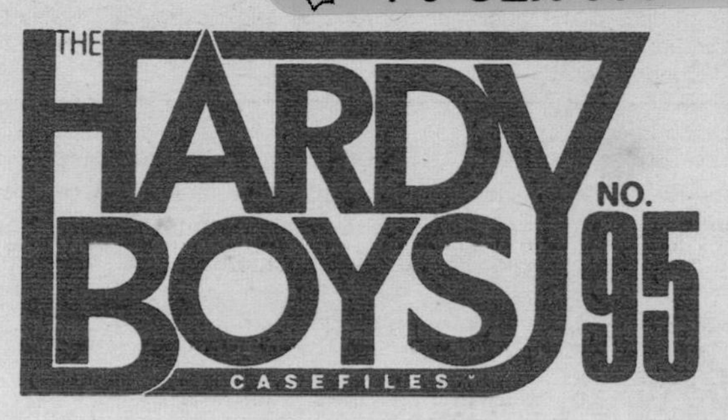

ILLEGAL PROCEDURE

FRANKLIN W. DIXON

AN ARCHWAY PAPERBACK
Published by POCKET BOOKS
New York London Toronto Sydney Tokyo Singapore

AN ARCHWAY PAPERBACK *Original*

An Archway Paperback published by
POCKET BOOKS, a division of Simon & Schuster Inc.
1230 Avenue of the Americas, New York, NY 10020

Produced by Mega-Books, Inc.

ISBN: 0-671-88206-6

First Archway Paperback printing January 1995

10 9 8 7 6 5 4 3 2 1

Cover art by Brian Kotzky

Printed in the U.S.A.

IL 6+

Chapter 1

"MINE!" JOE HARDY SHOUTED. The football tumbled end over end out of the sky. He gathered it to his chest and glanced upfield where his teammates were forming a blocking wall to the right. He angled in that direction, picking up speed.

One muscular defender broke through and was moving at an angle that would crowd Joe onto the sidelines. Joe shifted the ball to his outside arm, ran straight at the defender, then stopped short and cut toward the middle of the field. Unable to turn fast enough, his pursuer slapped only air as Joe sped by.

Joe felt as if he were flying. Only one man remained between him and the goal line. He faked a cut to the inside, but the other guy didn't go for it. So Joe began angling away from him, but the kid's long legs were quickly closing the distance between them.

Out of the corner of his eye, Joe sensed the arrival of a blocker. It was his lean-limbed older brother, Frank. He screened the defender away from Joe, who coasted past the goal line for the winning touchdown.

Shaking his blond hair from his eyes, Joe raised the ball high above his head and slammed it into the grass in a comical, exaggerated spike, then broke into a little victory dance.

His teammates crowded around to congratulate him. Some, like Joe, were in swimsuits. Others were sweating in short-legged wet suits. They slapped him on the back and grabbed him around the shoulders. So what if this was just a pickup game, Joe thought. The oceanfront park in San Diego was beautiful, and the beating of the surf on the rocks below was as thrilling as cheers from a crowd.

The kicker from the other team jogged over. "Good game, guys," he said. "That's about enough for us, though. We want to see how the Sharks do this afternoon against Atlanta." He looked over at Frank. "Are you going to be around next Sunday? We try to get a game in every weekend."

"We're not sure," Frank replied. "Our dad's here on business, and since it was our Christmas break we got to come along. But we may have to go back home to the East Coast before next weekend."

"To the snow," Joe added, with a mock shiver. "By this time next week we'll be shoveling the driveway."

The Hardys waved goodbye and walked across the street to the high-rise condominium where they were staying. The elevator shot them to the top floor. As the doors slid open, Joe started running down the empty hallway. "It's Hardy to the forty, the thirty, the twenty!" he shouted, zigzagging as he stiff-armed invisible tacklers.

Frank raced after him. Just as Joe shouted, "And Hardy scores!" Frank grabbed him and they fell against the door, which flew open. Joe and Frank went down in a heap at the feet of Fenton Hardy.

"Oh, hi, Dad," Joe managed to say. He glanced past his father at a man in white slacks, white deck shoes, and a navy blue yachting shirt who looked amused.

"Come in, boys," Fenton said. "I was just telling Mr. Chambers how mature and level-headed you are. Nicky, meet Frank and Joe."

Joe got to his feet and straightened his swim trunks. Was this really *the* Nicky Chambers, legendary owner of the San Diego Sharks? Now he recognized the tanned face, wavy white hair, and slow grin that he'd seen so often on television.

"It's a privilege to meet you, Mr. Chambers," Joe said, shaking the team owner's hand.

"Call me Nicky, boys," the man replied, turning to shake Frank's hand.

"Dad told us that his case had something to do with the Sharks," Frank remarked, running his hand back through his tousled brown hair. "But he wouldn't say what."

Fenton Hardy laughed. "You two go get cleaned up," he said. "When you come out, we'll fill you in."

Joe and Frank quickly showered and changed into shorts and T-shirts. Back in the living room their father and Nicky Chambers were talking on the sofa. The TV in the corner of the room was tuned to the Sharks-Generals game. The announcer was just reading the starting lineups.

Joe and Frank took chairs facing the two older men.

"Normally, I'd be there with the team," Chambers said. "But I'm afraid these aren't normal times for the Sharks."

Joe glanced over and caught Frank's gaze. They both knew that the Sharks were having a bad year. But what could the Hardys do about that?

Chambers stood up and walked over to the large window facing the ocean. "Things *started* going wrong when Bobby Walker died," he continued, his back to them. "Do you remember Bobby?"

Remember Bobby Walker? Joe thought. Who could forget him? He could still see the famous receiver's long, graceful stride, the ball settling into his arms as he glided by a frantic defender. Walker would have been a shoo-in for the Hall of Fame if he hadn't died in a car crash three years before.

"Since then," Chambers continued, returning to the sofa, "the team just hasn't played up to its potential. Everybody knows it. The media is taking potshots at us, and attendance is down."

"But you've got great players," Frank pointed out. "What about Elvin Jackson? And Racehorse Havranek?"

"Sure," Chambers said, "but they can't carry the team without Walker or another terrific receiver."

As if to confirm this assessment, a roar rose up from the TV. The Generals had just scored against the favored Sharks.

"Nicky suspects that the Sharks are being affected by something off the field," Fenton explained. "He's particularly concerned about a talent agency called Hyde-Ruskin, which represents a lot of the Sharks."

"Why?" Frank asked. "Embezzlement?"

Chambers stared down at his clasped hands. "I won't say that," he replied. "I simply feel that Peter Hyde has too much influence over my team. Look, I'll admit I'm old-fashioned. I don't like the way professional football has become big business, but it's a fact of life. A lot of players' careers don't last more than five years. A good agent like Hyde can double players' salaries from endorsement contracts. What can I do?"

"This guy Hyde," Joe said. "Did you ever talk to him about his influence over the players?"

"I've tried," Chambers said. "But he just laughs it off. I love the Sharks. The team has been like family to me. But if we can't turn things around, and quickly, I'll have to sell the team."

Joe was surprised at the older man's passion. "Where do we come in?" he asked.

Fenton Hardy said, "I'm going to have to move around a lot, between here, Washington, and Las Vegas. Peter Hyde is tied in with major players in those cities, too, which may turn out to be important. Meanwhile, we need someone inside at Hyde-Ruskin. Frank, I—"

Another roar from the TV set interrupted him. Chambers studied the screen, then rolled his eyes. The Generals were inside the Sharks' twenty-yard line.

"Third down and one at the nineteen!" the announcer said breathlessly. "The Sharks are pulled in tight. They have to stop this drive right here."

Joe watched the Generals' quarterback fake a throw into the line. The Sharks fell for it. The quarterback kept the ball, rolled to his left, and lofted a perfect spiral to his tight end, who was waiting all alone in the San Diego end zone. The Atlanta crowd went crazy. Nicky Chambers groaned.

"This shouldn't be happening," Chambers protested, as the Generals' kicker booted the ball between the goalposts for the extra point.

A commercial came on.

"As I was saying, Frank," Fenton said, "we need someone inside Hyde-Ruskin. Nicky asked Peter Hyde if, as a favor, he could find a spot in his mailroom for the son of an old friend, and Hyde agreed. You wouldn't mind going undercover, would you, Frank?"

"Not at all, Dad," Frank replied.

"What about me, Dad?" Joe asked.

"Well," Fenton said with an odd smile. He looked over at Chambers.

"Joe, how would you like to join the San Diego Sharks organization?" Chambers asked.

Joe stared at him, openmouthed. "Me, Mr. Chambers?" he said. "Join the Sharks?"

"That's right," Chambers said, smiling. "Your father and I had been talking about giving you a job, maybe as a trainer's assistant. But what I really need is someone who can tell me what's going on with the players, and that means someone who's one of them. I was watching you from the balcony a little while ago. You're not bad, son. What do you say to signing on as a second-string kick returner?"

Joe continued to stare at the team owner. Was he imagining this? Finally he jumped to his feet and gave a shout that rattled the glasses in the kitchen.

"I think that means yes," Fenton said dryly.

"Good," Chambers said. "But don't get too excited, Joe. I'm not saying we'll actually put you in a game. Sit down so we can talk details."

Joe was much too excited to focus on the discussion. From time to time he glanced at the TV screen. With five minutes to go, the Generals scored again, pulling to within three points of the Sharks.

"I'll be glad when this is over," Chambers said as the Generals lined up to kick off.

So near the end, Joe was expecting an onside kick. Instead, the Generals' kicker boomed one deep to "Hot Rod" Hill, the Sharks' talented young return man.

Hill took the ball at the goal line and headed upfield. At the ten, the Sharks' big defensive tackle, Ed "the House" McMaran, missed a block. Moments later Hill was smothered under an avalanche of red Generals jerseys. The ball spurted out of Hill's grasp and tumbled crazily into the end zone. A jubilant General fell on it for the go-ahead touchdown.

The camera panned back upfield to "Hot Rod" Hill. The star kick returner was still lying on the ground, his ankle twisted at a sickening angle.

Frank shook his head. "Looks like the Sharks are going to need to use their second-string returner. That means you, Joe."

Chapter 2

"NOW, HOLD ON," Fenton said, watching the first aid team carry the Sharks' kick returner off the field on a stretcher. "I can't allow Joe to run that kind of risk. What was I thinking of?"

"You're right, Fenton," the Sharks' owner said. "We'll have to come up with a different plan."

Joe saw his big chance disappearing as suddenly and unexpectedly as it had appeared. "But, Dad," he protested. "I—"

"Wait—how about a fair catch?" Frank said quickly. "If Joe called for a fair catch every time he fielded a kick, he wouldn't be tackled. Wouldn't that work, Mr. Chambers?"

Chambers nodded slowly. "It's an idea," he said.

Joe opened his mouth to protest, then abruptly closed it again. If he said no to Frank's suggestion, his father might nix the whole plan.

"What about Deke Landers?" Fenton asked, referring to the Sharks' outspoken head coach. "Will he go along?"

"He will if I explain why," Chambers said. "He's concerned about what's been happening, too."

Over the next half hour, Chambers and the three Hardys worked out the details of their plan. Finally Chambers stood up. "Joe, welcome to the Sharks," he said, offering his hand. "I'm grateful to you for being willing to help. I just hope we can get to the bottom of this while there's still some of the season left."

The next morning the Hardys were having breakfast on the balcony. Joe scanned a newspaper article about the Sharks' game against Atlanta, wincing at the sarcasm aimed at his new teammates.

Fenton Hardy finished his orange juice and glanced at his watch. "I've got a plane to catch," he announced. "I'll be in Washington and then in Las Vegas. I left you my number in both places, and I'll call to see how the two of you are as often as I can." He stood up and added, "But I want both of you to promise that you won't go looking for trouble."

Joe and Frank glanced at each other. "Sure, Dad," Frank said, answering for both of them.

A few minutes later Frank took the wheel of the cherry red convertible their father had rented. Joe wanted to relax and enjoy the view of the Pacific, but how could he? Just minutes from now he would have to walk into the dressing room of the San Diego Sharks to try to make a place for himself among sports legends. If only his shaky voice and sweaty palms didn't betray his nervousness!

Frank dropped him off in front of a door marked San Diego Sharks—Corporate Offices. Nicky Chambers was waiting for him in the owner's suite at the top of the stadium. The far wall of his office was all glass with an unobstructed view of the bright green playing field below. The opposite wall was also glass. Joe suddenly realized that it was one side of a huge aquarium. As he watched, a live shark—gray, sleek, and awesome—glided by.

"That's TD, our mako shark," Chambers said, nodding toward the aquarium. "He wanted to get a good look at you. And here's someone else who wants a look at you."

A middle-aged man with short red hair, a riot of freckles, and the flattened nose of an ex-boxer crossed the room.

"Meet Coach Landers," Chambers said. "Deke, this is Joe Hardy, the young man I've been telling you about."

The Sharks' head coach shook Joe's hand and in one glance sized him up. "Pleased to know you," Coach Landers said briskly.

"It's an honor," Joe said, trying not to wince at the coach's viselike grip. "I hope I can make a contribution to the team."

"Well, let's talk about that," Nicky Chambers said, leading Joe and Coach Landers to a circle of chairs near the aquarium. "Deke is as worried as I am about the problems we've been having. I told him about the fair-catch idea, and he's willing to go along with it."

Landers stared directly at Joe. "But I have to have your word that you'll follow my instructions to the letter, Joe," he said. "No hero stuff. Is that understood?"

"Yes, sir," Joe replied, swallowing. "I want to help the team any way I can."

"Good. I can tell we'll get along," Coach Landers responded.

Nicky smiled, and then stood up. "Now, how about introducing Joe to some of the guys?"

The coach nodded and rose. Joe followed him to the door, where the team owner gave him an encouraging pat on the back.

Joe and Coach Landers took the elevator down to the stadium's lower level, and then passed through a series of long halls until they arrived at the dressing room. As they walked through the door, Joe saw a stocky, blond guy in shorts and a T-shirt, sitting on a bench in a cubicle, scrawling his name on footballs with a felt-tip pen.

"Rich, meet Joe Hardy, our new punt-return man," Landers said. "Joe, this is Rich Havranek."

"Hi, kid," Havranek said. "We heard you were coming. You know this guy?" he added, nodding to a tall, slender man in the next cubicle. Joe nodded. He didn't need to look at the nameplate over the cubicle to recognize Elvin Jackson, one of the greatest quarterbacks in pro football.

"What do you say, man," Jackson greeted him. "Finding everything all right?"

"So far so good," Joe said, trying to sound cool. "See you later." He followed the coach across the crowded locker room.

Landers paused at a table where several team members were playing cards and said, "House, say hello to Joe Hardy."

Even sitting down, Ed "the House" McMaran was the biggest man Joe had ever seen. His sandy hair was shaved to a burr, and his neck was so thick it blended right into his shoulders.

Joe held out his hand to the red-faced giant, but McMaran merely nodded in his direction and kept studying his cards.

Coach Landers led Joe to a cubicle with a practice uniform and equipment. "This is yours," Landers said. "Today it's shorts and shoulder pads, just to limber up. I'll see you on the field in half an hour."

As Joe started changing, he glanced at the back of his jersey. Number Thirteen. Was somebody having a little fun with the rookie?

He noticed the cubicle next to his. Everything inside it was perfectly arranged—the white shoes and teal-colored stockings beside the silver helmet on the bench, black jersey and white game pants neatly hung on hooks. On the wall at the back of the cubicle was a color photograph of a slender, graceful receiver stretched full-length in midair, reaching for the football.

"Bobby Walker. He was the greatest," a voice behind him said. Joe turned to face a stocky, well-built man with a friendly smile and short black hair going gray. "I'm Carl Westcott," he said, holding out his hand.

"Joe Hardy," Joe said, amazed to be shaking the hand of "Crazy Legs" Westcott. Westcott had retired a decade before to join the Sharks' coaching staff, but he looked as if he could still run back a kickoff against the best in the game.

"You need anything, just ask," Westcott said. He glanced again at Bobby Walker's cubicle and shook his head sadly, before walking away.

Joe had just finished suiting up when he saw the other players start to head out. He followed them down the long tunnel that led to the sunlit playing field, all of their cleats clattering on the concrete walkway.

The team was put through a full hour of stretching exercises. A loping run to the fifty-yard line followed, then an exhausting series of wind sprints.

Finally Westcott blew his whistle and sent them to the showers. "Film room at two sharp," he added, to groans from the team. "Coach Landers wants to show you a horror movie."

Joe was on his way into the crowded, steamy shower when House McMaran slapped his shoulder.

"Hey, little buddy," the giant lineman growled. "A bunch of us are having dinner at the Neptune Room tonight. Want to come along?"

"Sure, great," Joe replied, pleased at the invitation and the chance to get to know his new teammates better.

The film of the Sharks-Generals game really was a horror show. Coach Landers lingered over every muffed assignment, every missed block, every dropped pass. Joe couldn't help feeling relieved that he hadn't been there.

"You're playing the Toros this Sunday," Landers reminded them. "You make any of these mistakes against them, they'll maul us. We'll be the laughingstock of the league."

When he came to House McMaran's missed block, the one that had cost the team the services of Hot Rod Hill, Landers was silent. But his silence spoke volumes. He ran the play over and over. Joe glanced at McMaran. Even in the gloom, he could see that the lineman's face was flushed and angry.

It was after five by the time the Sharks staggered out of the darkness of the film room. Joe assumed that McMaran would be too upset to follow through on the dinner invitation, but he was wrong. On the way out to the parking lot, the lineman came up behind him and gripped the back of Joe's neck with his ham-size hand.

"We'll take my heap," McMaran said, steering Joe toward a shiny black four-wheel drive vehicle that towered over the other cars on its monster tires.

It was a short ride up the coast to the restaurant, but McMaran drove like a maniac. Joe didn't relax his death grip on the armrest until they pulled into the parking lot. Then, looking around, he realized that they weren't that far from their condo. He'd have to bring Frank here some night.

The Neptune Room was a rambling redwood building on a hillside that sloped down to the ocean. The entrance was at street level, but the back of the restaurant was built out over the water on pilings. Inside, Joe was astonished to see waves crashing against the giant picture window at the far end of the room.

Jackson, Havranek, and six or eight other Sharks were already at a long table near the window. Joe sat down next to Havranek, but he couldn't take his eyes off the surf only a few feet from his chair.

Havranek grinned at him. "It's something, isn't it?" he said. "A couple of times the waves have gotten big enough to break the window. They've got photos out in the lobby."

McMaran started tapping his knife on his water glass. Nobody noticed. Suddenly he slammed his fist onto the tabletop and shouted, "HEY, JERKS!" The whole restaurant fell silent.

McMaran gazed at Joe. Joe felt his heart skip a beat.

"Little buddy, it's a tradition that rookies have to sing for their supper," McMaran said. "So up on the table, and give us your school song."

"Sing! Sing! Sing!" his teammates chanted, pounding the table and making the plates rattle.

Joe froze. What school song? Obviously they all thought he'd been to college. But before he could protest, the players on either side of him grabbed his arms and lifted him onto the table.

Suddenly he recalled the Bayport High

School fight song, set to the tune of "Cheer, Cheer for Old Notre Dame."

"Cheer, cheer for old Bayport U," he croaked, changing the words as he went along. Recognizing the tune, others in the restaurant started singing along. That made it easier. By the time he got to "And march on to victory!" he was waving his arms and directing them.

Cheers came from all around. Joe grinned and took a bow, then straightened up in time to see Frank walk in—with a beautiful blond girl. When Frank spotted Joe, his jaw dropped. Then he grinned and beckoned.

Joe clambered down from the table and started across the room toward Frank and his companion.

"Hi," he said. "I was just—"

Still grinning, Frank said, "We saw. Sandy, this is my talented little brother, Joe. Joe, meet Sandy Sharpe. We work together."

"Lucky you," Joe started to say. But suddenly he was shoved to one side.

"I want to meet this little lady," House McMaran told Frank. He reached for Sandy's arm.

"Come on, House," Joe said. "You can't—"

"Keep out of this," House growled. "Well, little honey, what's your name?"

"Now, hold on, fella—" Frank started to say. But McMaran put his huge paw on Frank's face and shoved him to the floor. Frank scrambled up and took a swing at McMaran, but the giant swatted him away as if he were a gnat.

The girl backed away, horror-struck. As McMaran reached for her again, she suddenly crouched and spun on one foot. With the other foot, she lashed out with lightning speed at McMaran's throat. "Hai-yaa!" she shouted as the blow landed.

"Urgh!" McMaran grunted. He stumbled backward against a table. Then, enraged, he picked up the table, scattering the plates and cutlery like dry leaves. Raising it high over his head, he flung it in the direction of Frank and the girl.

It missed. Joe gasped as the heavy table slammed into the huge window, which was instantly covered with thousands of spiderweb cracks. Seconds later when the next wave came, the glass gave way. The ocean flooded in with a roar.

Joe watched, astounded, as tables, chairs, and screaming people were carried helplessly into the darkness by the outrushing sea. Then he felt himself being sucked out through the broken window. He searched desperately for something to hold on to.

"Frank!" Joe shouted. "Help!"

He choked as salt water filled his mouth. Then everything went black.

Chapter 3

FRANK MADE A GRAB for Sandy as the freezing water sucked them out of the building into the open sea. Around them in the darkness, frantic voices called out for help. Frank kicked off his shoes and helped Sandy ride a wave in to shore.

"Are you okay?" Frank asked her.

"Sure," she said. Her teeth chattered from the cold. "I could sure use some coffee, though. I wonder where that waiter went."

Frank laughed and rubbed her back to warm her up. Then the two of them waded back into the water to help others to shore. Three police cruisers raced up, sirens blaring, and aimed their searchlights at the bay. Two ambulances and a yellow beach patrol truck followed. The lifeguards and emergency squad members pulled on wet suits and raced toward the water.

Frank stood knee-deep in the surf and scanned the area for Joe. Where was he? Joe was a superb swimmer, but as the minutes passed, Frank began to worry. He watched as House McMaran floated in to shore like a beached whale. Two police officers were waiting for him at the edge of the surf. As they strained to lift him out of the water, several TV news crews moved in.

The headwaiter of the restaurant came over in his dripping tux to ask Frank and Sandy to give the police statements about what had happened.

"Have you seen the young guy who was with the Sharks, the one who was singing on the table?" Frank asked him.

"No," the headwaiter said, "but the cops are making a list of everyone who was in there. Maybe they can help you."

As he wandered back toward the ruined restaurant, Frank heard him mutter, "We'll never let another Shark in the place again!"

Someone slipped blankets around their shoulders. After telling the police what they knew, Frank and Sandy paced up and down the water's edge, searching for Joe. Frank's mood grew increasingly grim.

"I think I'd better phone Dad," he said after

half an hour. "Our condo's not far from here. You can call your mother from there, and we'll find you something dry to put on."

The sports car was where Frank had parked it. They got in and drove along the seafront boulevard. Suddenly Frank hit the brakes. There in the headlights was a bedraggled, barefoot figure in a soaked tennis shirt and khakis. He was holding out his thumb, hitching back to the scene of the accident.

"Joe!" Frank shouted, not hiding the joy and relief he felt as he pulled over to the shoulder of the road. "Where have you been?"

"I went for a swim," Joe replied with a tired grin. "How about a lift back, so the police'll know I'm accounted for."

Joe squeezed into the tiny backseat of the convertible, and Frank let out the clutch.

Half an hour later they were pulling into the basement garage of the condominium complex. The three of them took the elevator up to the apartment.

"So what happened to you?" Frank asked as he and Joe changed. Sandy was in Fenton's room, slipping into the jeans and sweatshirt Frank had found for her.

"I'm not really sure," Joe replied. "I remember being swept through the window and going under, and then something hit me on the head. The next thing I knew, I was a long way from the restaurant. I swam for shore, but it was really rocky where I landed. That must be where I got this," he added, gingerly touching a red welt over his left eyebrow.

"What then?" Frank asked.

Joe shrugged. "I walked along the edge of the surf until I found a place where I could climb up to the street. Then you guys came along. By the way, I like your new friend."

"Sandy's mother is Clarissa Sharpe, president of the Mercury Shoe Company. She got Sandy a job at Hyde-Ruskin 'cause so many athletes signed with Hyde-Ruskin endorse Mercury shoes. She's in the mailroom with me. Come on, let's go make some hot chocolate."

As Frank poured milk into a saucepan, Sandy came out into the living room. She was barefoot and had brushed her wet hair straight back. Frank thought she was even prettier that way.

"I used the phone in the bedroom to call my mom," Sandy told them. "She's coming right over."

At the mention of Sandy's mother, Joe remembered the Mercury commercial with Elvin Jackson in a T-shirt, jeans, and white Mercury cross-trainers, racing triumphantly to the top of a sand dune. It made every kid in America want a pair of Mercs. In his mind, Joe saw a new commercial. This time Elvin had a companion—Joe Hardy, ace punt returner for the San Diego Sharks.

Frank carried the steaming pan and three mugs to the coffee table in the living room. Joe shook himself and followed.

Sandy poured herself a cup of hot chocolate and took a sip, then said, "So what's your friend's problem, Joe?"

"House McMaran? He's no friend of mine," Joe replied. "The guy's obviously a jerk. When he saw you, something must have snapped. He went completely ballistic."

A buzzer sounded from the lobby downstairs. Frank listened to the intercom, then said, "Come on up, Ms. Sharpe." A few minutes later, he opened the door to an attractive woman in a blue knit dress and heels who could almost have passed for Sandy's older sister.

"From what I heard on the radio coming over here, you kids have had quite a night," she said, giving her daughter a hug. "Frank, I'm pleased to meet you."

"And, Mom, this is Joe," Sandy said. "Frank's brother. He's just joined the Sharks."

"Really? Congratulations, Joe," Melissa Sharpe said, shaking Joe's hand. "I work with several of your new teammates. They help me sell Mercury shoes."

Frank handed her a cup of hot chocolate and said, "I've always wondered how that works."

"Thank you," Melissa said, taking a sip of

her drink and leaning back on the couch. "Endorsements, you mean?"

Frank nodded.

"Simple, really," she replied. "We've found that sports stars sell athletic shoes. After we signed Elvin Jackson three years ago, our sales jumped twenty percent. So we can afford to pay our athletes a lot of money. It's a mutually beneficial arrangement."

Joe was slouched low in his chair, his legs stretched out in front of him. He studied his well-worn Mercurys. "Hey, I'd do it for a new pair of Mercs," he said with a grin. "How about signing *me* up?"

Melissa smiled. "Who knows?" she replied. "We'll see what kind of season you have, then talk again. But right now, I want to get my little half-drowned kitten home to bed." She ran a hand through her daughter's damp hair.

"See you bright and early, Frank," Sandy said as she and her mother stood up. "You know what they say—neither sleet nor snow nor flooded restaurants can keep the mail from going through."

Frank and Joe laughed.

"Say, Sandy," Joe said as they all walked to the door. "I saw how you put away McMaran with that awesome kick. Where'd you learn to be a Ninja warrior?"

"In Japan, where else?" Sandy replied. "Mom headed up Mercury's Japanese subsidiary for five years. I took up karate while we were there and earned my black belt three years ago."

After the Sharpes left, Joe said, "Some girl. No offense, Frank, but what's she doing in the mailroom?"

"Like I said, learning the business," Frank replied. "She's majoring in international business at the university. The job at Hyde-Ruskin is only part-time, just to give her some practical experience. I get the feeling that her mother and Peter Hyde are friends."

"How about you? Are you learning anything about the company?" Joe asked.

"Not too much," Frank replied. "But it was just my first day. Sandy did tell me that the guy who handles the Sharks' accounts is named Rosen. Andrew Rosen."

Joe carried the mugs and cocoa pan back to the kitchen, then slid open the glass door to the balcony. Frank joined him. They stared out at the ebony ocean, glistening in the light of a quarter moon.

"Listen, what's with that guy McMaran?" Frank asked. "What happened tonight was really scary."

Joe shook his head. "I don't know. He didn't much like watching himself foul up during the film session today, but that doesn't explain the way he acted. Maybe he's on something. I wouldn't mind finding out what."

Frank glanced at his watch. "Just about time for the news," he remarked. "Let's see how the local stations cover the freestyle swimming event at the Neptune Room."

Joe followed Frank inside and clicked on the remote.

"Near tragedy tonight at a popular oceanside restaurant on La Jolla Cove," the announcer was saying. Behind him pictures of the flooded restaurant appeared. Frank caught a glimpse of himself and Sandy talking to a police officer.

"Six people were treated for exposure at Scripps Hospital, but fortunately no one was seriously injured," the newscaster continued. "Witnesses say the incident was the result of roughhousing by members of the San Diego Sharks. Taken into custody was Ed 'The House' McMaran, all-pro offensive tackle for the Sharks. Bail has been set at ten thousand dollars."

Frank and Joe watched another officer putting a handcuffed McMaran into the backseat of a patrol car. Then a grim Nicky Chambers came on, telling an interviewer that he was deeply ashamed. "There will be heavy fines," he said. "You can count on it."

"No real harm done," a man in an expensive suit and flashy tie told another interviewer. The caption identified him as McMaran's attorney. "The fellows were just blowing off steam, and they got a little carried away. My client will be more than happy to pay for any damages."

As the newscast shifted to a story from Europe, Frank shook his head and glanced over at his brother. "I don't care if they are professional athletes," he said disgustedly. "Those guys need to grow up."

"Don't look at me," Joe said, clicking off the TV. "I'm doing my best to be mature. And one thing that means is no late shows for me. A pro athlete needs his sleep."

Joe didn't have to be at practice until two P.M. the next day, so Frank was up well before him. He drank his orange juice and scanned the morning paper. The Neptune Room incident had made the front page, and the sports section was full of scathing comments from Nicky Chambers, Deke Landers, and other members of the Sharks' staff.

As Frank drove to work, he thought about the day's priorities. Number one was to find out more about Andrew Rosen, who dealt directly with the Sharks. But what about Melissa Sharpe? If she was a friend of Hyde, she might also be tied in to what was troubling the Sharks. And in that case, could he trust Melissa Sharpe's daughter?

That morning as he and Sandy were sorting the mail, he said casually, "What's with this guy Rosen? He gets more mail than anyone."

Sandy laughed. "Handy Andy? He handles the Sharks' accounts. I don't know that the players like him very much, but he negotiates very juicy contracts for them with athletic shoe companies, pizza chains, soft drink companies—you name it. He makes a bundle for them."

"Do you know him?" Frank asked.

"Not really," Sandy said with a shrug. "I've seen him at parties. He's kind of nervous and whiny, but he puts up a front to make you think he's more important than he really is."

Later, when an overnight package arrived that needed Rosen's signature, Frank took it up to his sixth-floor office and gave it to Rosen's secretary. Through the open office door, he heard someone, apparently Rosen, talking on the phone. Frank turned his back and pretended to study the autographed photos on the wall while he listened.

"Does the Syndicate have a line on him?" he heard Rosen ask.

There was a short silence.

Then Rosen said, "Joe Hardy, huh?" He chuckled nervously and continued. "Yes, I understand. Don't worry. We always get our man."

Chapter 4

FRANK STOOD rooted to the floor. The talent agent had to be talking about Joe, he thought.

"Is there anything else?" Rosen's secretary demanded, startling Frank. He turned and took a signed receipt from her. "No, that's it," he said as cheerfully as he could. "See you later."

As he walked to the elevator, he wondered who the Syndicate was and why it wanted Rosen to "take care of" his younger brother. One thing was sure—Rosen hadn't sounded friendly.

After a shower and a sandwich, Joe took a cab to the stadium. When he entered the dressing room he could tell immediately that his fellow players were in shock. Even those who hadn't been at the Neptune Room the night before were upset and deeply embarrassed. They had seen the newscasts and read the papers. Even though House McMaran was the only player who had ended up in jail, the incident had given the whole team a terrible black eye.

A deep silence fell over the locker room as Deke Landers walked in.

"What are you? A bunch of juvenile delinquents?" he demanded, pacing back and forth in the center of the room. "Well, I've got news for you. In case you didn't notice, you're grown men. You're role models for kids all over this country. Some role models!"

Landers paused to stare at his players. Suddenly he slapped his clipboard down on the desk. It sounded like a rifle shot. "Every single one of you who was at that restaurant last night is going to pay. Nicky Chambers will set the amounts, but believe me, your wallets are going to be a lot lighter after this."

He turned to Joe. "And that means you, too, Hardy," he said. "I don't care if it was your first day on the team. You should have known better."

Joe wanted to sink through the floor. He hoped Coach Landers didn't really mean it. After all, how could he be fined when he wasn't even being paid?

"On the field in fifteen minutes," Coach

Landers added with a grim face. "You all have a little running to do."

Half an hour later Joe was envying Frank. The coach had put them through ten hundred-yard and fifteen fifty-yard sprints—and that was just for openers.

Next came a fiendish drill called running the lines. The players lined up at the goal line, then, at the whistle, sprinted to the ten-yard line, touched it, ran back to the goal line, touched it, sprinted to the twenty-yard line, touched it—over and over, until they had run to the fifty-yard line and back.

By the time they finished, Joe and his teammates were in agony, their chests heaving and their breath coming in raspy gasps.

"Okay, men, now we're going to get down to business," Coach Landers shouted through a bullhorn. "We've got a tough game coming up on Sunday against the Toros."

The Sharks broke into offensive and defensive units and retreated to opposite ends of the field. Crazy Legs Westcott gathered his punt returner and the kickoff receivers around him.

"Here's what I want you to do," he said. "Take a ball and wait for Bobby Joe to punt. As soon as he puts the ball in the air, you play catch with the one you're holding. Like this."

Westcott picked up a ball and shouted, "Kick one, B. J."

Downfield the team's punter got off a high,

spiraling kick. The coach circled under the punted ball, all the while tossing *his* ball up and down. When the punted ball came down, Westcott was waiting to catch it with his free arm.

"Okay, your turn, Hardy," Westcott said.

Joe felt his stomach buckle. He was sure he was about to make a fool of himself. Still, he picked up a ball and began tossing and catching it, as Westcott had done. B. J. kicked one that sailed high into the blue. Joe's instincts took over. He *knew* where the ball would come down. When it did, he was right under it and caught it easily.

"Attaway, my man!" Coach Westcott shouted. "You guys see that?"

"Nice catch, kid," Rich Havranek said, giving Joe a friendly slap on the fanny.

Joe tried not to let his relief and pleasure show.

For the next two hours they worked on recognizing Toro offensive and defensive alignments. Then they ran more sprints. When Coach Landers finally called an end to practice, Joe could barely put one foot in front of the other.

He was stripping off his sweat-soaked jersey when one of the trainers came over. "Doc Washington wants to see you before you go," he said.

"Who's that?" Joe groaned.

"The conditioning coach," the trainer replied. "Right down the hall."

Joe felt better after a hot shower, but he was still hobbling when he walked into Washington's office. She was a tall, dark-skinned woman in a teal-colored warmup suit. "I hear it was tough out there today," she said.

"It sure was," Joe replied. "I hope you called me in here to issue me a new body. This old one's worn out."

Washington gave a small smile. "Not quite," she said. "But I am going to give you a diet and a training routine to get you through a long, grueling season."

She handed him two computer printouts, one listing the food groups he should be eating and the other detailing the stretching and lifting exercises he was to do every day. After going over them with him, she gave him what looked like a prescription and said, "We use a little pharmacy in Ocean Beach, not far from here. Get this filled there right away."

Joe glanced at the piece of paper. He couldn't make out a word. "What's it for?" he asked.

"Special diet supplements to help you bulk up without getting fat," Washington replied.

Joe frowned. "I'm not much for pills. I'll just rely on exercise and chocolate malts and plenty of rest, if you don't mind."

"I do mind," Washington snapped. "I'm responsible for this team's conditioning, and as long as you're under contract to the Sharks, you'll do as I say. Do I make myself clear?"

Joe saluted. "Loud and clear," he said. "I'll get it filled this afternoon."

A little later Joe was standing outside the stadium, waiting for Frank to pick him up, when he saw Washington come out with quarterback Elvin Jackson. They looked as if they were arguing about something. Joe caught the words *new guy*. Then they noticed him and fell silent.

At that moment Frank drove up and stopped at the curb nearby. Joe gave Jackson and Washington a casual wave and climbed in.

As Frank pulled away, he said, "You're getting famous around here." He related what he had heard in Rosen's office that morning.

"Maybe he wants to arrange a big endorsement contract for me," Joe suggested.

"Whatever he's arranging, I get the feeling you won't like it," Frank replied. "Don't worry, though, I'll keep an eye on him."

Joe sat back and enjoyed the breeze. After a couple of minutes, he asked, "Where are we headed?"

"I'm meeting Sandy for dinner at a pasta place on the beach," Frank told him. "Want to come?"

Joe glanced at him with his eyebrows raised teasingly. "Well, if I won't be in the way . . ."

"Put a lid on it," his older brother shot back.

Joe laughed, then said. "Listen, can we stop by a drugstore in Ocean Beach?"

"Sure, after we pick up Sandy," Frank said. "Catch a cold from your dip in the ocean last night?"

"Nope. I've just got to fill a prescription the conditioning coach gave me," Joe replied.

Sandy was waiting in front of her apartment building when they arrived.

"Hi, guys," she said brightly. Joe wedged his tired body into the cramped backseat so she could sit up front with Frank.

Frank found Joe's pharmacy, but not a parking place. "Hop out. We'll go around the block and pick you up right here."

When Frank and Sandy came back around, Joe was still inside. There was no traffic, so Frank pulled up next to a parked car and put the gear lever in neutral.

They'd been waiting less than a minute when Frank heard a throaty rumble from behind him. It sounded like an army tank. He looked over his shoulder to see a huge black 4 × 4 rolling up the street toward them. At the wheel was House McMaran.

Sandy glanced around, too, and groaned. "I heard on the radio that he was out on bail," she commented.

Just then House spotted them and screeched to a halt. "Uh-oh," Frank murmured as the giant lineman climbed down out of the cab and stomped up to his side of the car. Frank gently slid the gear lever into first.

House bent over until his red face was just inches from Frank. "Out of that car, you little jerk," he growled. "You're the reason I spent last night in the slammer." Then he looked over at Sandy, his lips twisted in a sneer. "And I want to have a word with little Wonder-woman over there, too."

"Sure, House, sure," Frank said mildly. "Take it easy. Just give me some room. I'll get out and we can talk this over like adults."

McMaran straightened up. Instantly Frank pressed the accelerator to the floor and popped the clutch. The powerful little sports car left two tracks of rubber as it leapt forward.

"I think Joe's going to have to find his own way home," Frank murmured.

He glanced in the mirror. House was racing back to his 4 × 4. A moment later the giant vehicle jerked into motion, forcing a delivery truck to swerve to keep from hitting it.

"See if you can lose him on some of those little streets by the beach," Sandy suggested. Frank nodded and made a quick right onto a narrow residential lane, but McMaran stayed right behind them.

"I'll get on Pacific Coast Highway," Frank said. "Maybe we can outrun him. I hope so. If he catches us, he'll probably roll that monster truck right over us."

They headed up the beachside highway with McMaran close behind. A few times he tried to change lanes and pull up beside them, but Frank's weaving kept him at bay.

"I've got an idea," Sandy said, looking back at their pursuer. "Get ready to exit at Torrey Pines Road—it's coming right up."

Frank waited until he was nearly past the exit, then downshifted to third, gave the brakes a hard tap, and jerked the wheel to the right, putting the agile, racing-bred convertible into a four-wheel drift onto the exit ramp. McMaran was going too fast to make the sudden turn, but Frank had no doubt he'd be back.

"Pull in here," Sandy told Frank a couple of minutes later, pointing to a dusty parking area rimmed with eucalyptus trees. The sign at the entrance said San Diego Hang Glider Port.

"Come with me," she commanded as Frank stopped the car beside a little frame shack at the edge of a cliff that overlooked the ocean. Frank could see several people holding long, brightly colored triangular wings, standing at the edge of the cliff.

"Huh-uh, no way," Frank said, as he realized what Sandy had in mind.

"There's no time to argue," Sandy said.

"Don't worry, I'm an instructor here. Just do what I tell you, and you'll be fine."

She led him over to a couple of the wing sets lying on the ground near the edge of the cliff. "This is the control bar," she said, picking up the light nylon and aluminum contraption. "And these are the downtubes. You steer by shifting your weight. You get into the harness while I go for your helmet and parachute."

"*Parachute!* Not a chance! I'm out of here." Frank put down the hang glider and started back toward the car.

"Suit yourself," Sandy said. "I guess you'd rather wait here and have House McMaran throw you off the cliff, *without* a parachute."

At that he stopped and turned back. She had her hands on her hips and was smiling, with her blond hair flying in the wind.

"Don't worry," she added. "I'll be right alongside you."

She went off. Frank shrugged and picked up the hang glider. When Sandy returned with the helmets and parachute packs, she helped him into his harness, then got herself ready.

"Okay," she said. "I'll count three. Take a deep breath, run downhill to the edge of the cliff, and let the wind take over."

She began counting. Frank closed his eyes and opened them just in time to see McMaran's giant Jeep bouncing into the parking lot, a trail of red dust billowing up behind it.

The sight of the huge, enraged football player was all it took to send Frank trotting down the hill beside his new friend. He felt heavy and awkward. But suddenly the wind caught the wings and he was airborne. He shouted with joy and relief as he soared out over the Pacific.

As he and Sandy wheeled and soared like hawks, Frank peered down on McMaran's 4 × 4 far below. The big man had gotten out and walked over to the shack at the cliff's edge. He seemed to have no idea that Frank and Sandy were right above him. Frank wished he had brought along a water balloon.

Frank gestured to Sandy, and they watched McMaran talk to a couple of people, then walk over to the red convertible. Frank was afraid he might push the car off the cliff, but maybe there were too many people around for that. He returned to his 4 × 4, got in, and sped away.

Relieved, Frank turned to Sandy and pointed toward the ground. She nodded. He shifted his weight against the downtube, as Sandy had instructed, but suddenly he felt himself caught by a downdraft. He pulled hard on the control bar, trying to lift the nose of the glider, but nothing happened. To his horror, he saw that he was heading straight toward the face of the cliff. He was as helpless as a bug about to be smashed against a car windshield.

Chapter 5

The dark face of the cliff loomed nearer. Frank shut his eyes tightly and held his breath. At the very last second the wind seemed to take pity on him, catching his wings and lifting him upward. Moments later he was landing on top of the cliff.

Sandy landed nearby. "Wasn't that fun?" she called as she unbuckled her harness.

Frank realized that she had no idea how close he had come to crashing into the cliff. "It had its moments," he said dryly.

Shortly after that, the two of them were back on the Pacific Coast Highway. When they arrived at the condo, they found Joe sprawled on the couch.

"What happened to you guys?" he demanded, sitting up. "I figured you'd gone to dinner without me."

Frank and Sandy took turns relating their adventure. Then Sandy called out for an extra large deep-dish pizza.

"That McMaran is something else," she said when she returned from the phone. "You think he'll come here for us?"

"I doubt it," Joe said. "His rages seem to come and go. Which reminds me." He reached into his jeans pocket and pulled out a small plastic bottle. Removing the cap, he spilled out several large white tablets.

"Do either of you know what these are?" he asked.

"Sure," Frank said. "Pills. Okay, okay, what are they?" he added, as Joe picked up a pillow from the sofa and threatened to throw it.

"According to the pharmacist, they're steroids," Joe replied.

"Aren't those illegal?" Sandy asked.

"Not illegal," Frank told her. "But they are banned from professional sports. They're dangerous."

"Why?" she asked. "What do they do to you?"

"They make you think you can leap tall buildings in a single bound," Frank replied. "And they really do make people stronger. That's why weight lifters, football players, even high school athletes take a chance on using them. But they also can destroy your liver, break down your kidneys."

"And mess up your head, sending you into 'roid rages," Joe added. "That's another reason they're banned in every sport."

"Scary," Sandy said.

The buzzer sounded from the lobby. Joe went to the intercom, then announced, "It's the pizza." Sandy and Frank set out plates and glasses while Joe answered the door and brought the box to the table.

The pizza went quickly. As he finished his third slice, Joe said, "You know, steroids would explain a lot about the way House McMaran's been acting—and maybe some of the others on the team. But I can't help feeling there's more going on. I wouldn't be surprised if this steroid business leads us somewhere else."

Joe caught a warning glance from Frank and realized that he might have said too much in front of Sandy. Had she noticed?

"Somewhere else is where I'd better go," Sandy said, yawning. "After all this excitement, I've got to get some sleep."

Frank drove her home. When he got back, Joe was still up. As Frank slid onto the couch, Joe commented, "I keep forgetting she's Melissa Sharpe's daughter. That's what that look you gave me meant, right?"

"Well—if you ask me, I think Sandy's terrific," Frank said. "But we don't know much about her mother, or how Sandy gets along with her. We'd probably be smart not to let her know what we're doing."

Joe stretched out and let out a hollow groan. "I'm going to take a hot bath, then hit the sack," he announced. "I bet I'll be running plays in my dreams."

Joe was still asleep when Frank left for work the next morning. As Frank drove downtown, he realized that he was really looking forward to seeing Sandy.

The mailroom of Hyde-Ruskin was in a windowless space in the basement. Frank and Sandy stood at a large worktable, sorting letters and packages. As usual, Andrew Rosen had one of the largest stacks of mail. Frank was determined to find out more about him. But how?

The day before, as he was knocking off work, Frank had noticed the nighttime cleaning staff stopping by a small room just down the hall from the mailroom. Now, as he pushed a trolley of mail down the hall, he saw that the door to the room was open. He glanced inside. On the wall was a large metal cabinet that looked like a fuse box. The cabinet was open, and inside, on hooks, were dozens of shiny brass keys, arranged by floor and office number.

Frank saw his chance. Glancing quickly up and down the hall, he ducked inside, found the key to Rosen's office, and pocketed it. During his lunch hour, he drove to a hardware store and had a copy made, then spent the afternoon watching for a chance to replace the original. It finally came as the cleaning crew began to arrive and someone left the box open.

Frank drove by the stadium after work, where Joe was waiting for him. He seemed out of sorts.

"What's wrong?" Frank asked. "Did the House fall on you?"

"No," Joe said. "But he was there today, and he was not a happy camper. According to the scuttlebutt, Nicky fined him close to fifty thousand dollars. I steered clear of the guy."

"Was practice hard?" Frank asked.

"Not really," Joe replied. "We spent a lot of time working on the kind of plays the Toros tend to run. But Coach Landers called me into his office after practice to remind me about our fair-catch agreement."

Joe slapped the dashboard in frustration. "I know he's just trying to keep me safe but, Frank, I can play with those guys, I *know* I can."

Frank glanced at his brother's determined face. "Hey, your day will come," he said. They waited at an intersection while a bright red bus marked Tijuana bustled by. "Just enjoy yourself. Which reminds me, how about a game of hide-and-seek tonight?"

Joe gave him an unbelieving look. "A *what?"* he demanded.

"Hide as in H-Y-D-E," Frank said with a grin. He produced the key from his pocket. "This opens Andrew Rosen's office."

"All right!" Joe exclaimed.

It was after dark when Joe and Frank drove back downtown. The sidewalks were empty, and a fog was drifting in from the bay. They parked a couple of blocks from the Hyde-Ruskin building, and Frank led the way to the alley at the rear. Suddenly Frank grabbed Joe's arm and pulled him deeper into the shadows.

A bright rectangle appeared in the back wall, as someone pushed open a door and stepped outside—one of the cleaning staff getting a breath of fresh air, Frank realized. After a few moments the man went back inside, but a slit of light indicated that he hadn't completely closed the door.

"Even better than I hoped," Frank whispered as he and Joe crept into the building. "I thought we'd have to pick the lock."

"Got the camera?" Joe asked as they rode the elevator to the sixth floor.

"Right here," Frank said, taking a powerful miniature camera from his jacket pocket.

The elevator door slid open. Quietly Frank and Joe walked down the carpeted hall to Rosen's office. Frank inserted the key in the outer door and stepped inside. Joe, right behind him, closed the door tightly and switched on the light. Frank was already at the inner door. He took a deep breath. Would the same key open both doors?

It did. Frank pushed the door open. Rosen's desk was in the middle of the room, with a computer on a small table next to it. Behind the desk were large, old-fashioned casement windows with a view of the San Diego skyline and the bay.

Frank nodded toward two tall file cabinets in the corner. "You check the files," he said. "I'll try to hack into his computer."

The files on the Sharks were right where they should be, under *S*. Joe pulled them out and asked Frank for the camera, then spread out the papers on a table and began to photograph them, page by page.

"Ha!" Frank exclaimed, just as Joe was finishing. "Guess what Rosen's password is—*Killer*. As in killer shark, I guess. Some smart dude, huh?"

Frank file-surfed for a few minutes. Then Joe saw him sit up straighter and lean toward the computer screen. "This is interesting," Frank said. "Give me a glance at those papers you found."

Joe put a few files on the desk next to Frank. The older Hardy thumbed through them, then stared at the computer again.

"It looks to me as if Handy Andy is keeping a second set of files on the Sharks here," Frank commented.

"A backup, you mean?" Joe peered over his brother's shoulder. He soon saw what had drawn Frank's attention. The numbers on paper showed the amount that the Mercury Shoe Company was paying the Sharks' team players represented by Hyde-Ruskin. The figures in Rosen's computer showed the amount the Sharks actually received. There was a very big difference, and it wasn't in the football players' favor.

"Can you believe it?" Frank said, scrolling down the file. "The guy's skimming money that's supposed to go to the Sharks—"

The sound of a key in the outer door made Frank break off, eyes wide.

"Quick," Frank whispered. "We can't be found here!" He looked around desperately, but there was only the one door. They were trapped.

"Outside," Frank said, pushing his brother toward the window. "Don't worry, there's a ledge," he added, turning the crank.

"What about you?" Joe demanded, as he climbed onto the windowsill.

"I'll bluff," Frank said, hoping he sounded more confident than he felt.

Joe gave him a last worried look, then stepped out onto the ledge, six floors above the street. An instant later the door banged open. Frank spun around. Andrew Rosen was standing in the doorway with an efficient-looking automatic in his hand—aimed directly at Frank's chest.

Chapter 6

"PUT YOUR HANDS on the desk," Rosen said, his voice trembling. He was a short man with thinning hair and glasses. "What are you doing in my office?"

Frank saw the pistol shaking in the man's grasp, and realized the danger he was in. What if Rosen, in a panic, accidentally squeezed the trigger?

"Take it easy," Frank said, keeping his voice calm and soothing. "It's okay. I'm from the Syndicate." The words just popped out. He had no idea what the Syndicate meant to Rosen. But he saw the surprise on Rosen's face. The man began to lower the gun, then changed his mind and again pointed it straight at Frank.

Frank kept talking, relieved that Rosen had not recognized him as one of the mailroom employees. "Sorry we had to audit you this way, but, hey, it's the price of doing business. Now be a good sport and put the gun away."

Rosen slowly lowered the gun. Frank wondered why he was carrying it in the first place.

"What do you want with me?" Rosen asked in a voice tinged with fear.

Frank, still standing behind Rosen's desk, realized that whatever the Syndicate was, Rosen was afraid of it. To keep him off balance, Frank sat down in the man's chair and propped a foot up on his desk. He hoped Rosen wouldn't wonder about the breeze whipping the curtains at the open window behind him.

"Sit down," he said.

"Look," Rosen pleaded. "I'm in a little trouble. I need time, that's all."

He put the gun down on the desk, not far from Frank, and seemed glad to be rid of it.

Frank remained silent as he slid the automatic away from the agent. "Anyway, these figures tell me you've been doing some skimming for your own benefit." He pushed the papers Joe had found toward Rosen.

"That's not true," Rosen said, panic rising in his voice. He picked up the papers and began shuffling through them. "Everything here is strictly what we agreed to. Mr. Hyde knows that."

"Mr. Hyde doesn't know that," Frank said, noting that Rosen's panic seemed to increase with the mention of Peter Hyde. "And by the way, why do you carry a gun?"

Rosen blanched. "Look—I gamble, for high stakes," he blurted out. "I need to protect myself, that's all. It doesn't have anything to do with Mr. Hyde."

Frank would have loved to hear more about Mr. Hyde, but he was afraid of pushing his luck. "Okay," he said, "here's the deal. You go home. I'll report back, and you'll be hearing from us. I'll hang on to the gun."

Rosen hesitated, then walked toward the door. Frank waited to hear the outer door close, then took a deep breath.

On the narrow ledge outside, Joe was pressing his back against the rough white stucco and trying not to look down at the street below. A sea gull made a two-point landing beside him. The big white bird seemed perfectly comfortable on the ledge. Why not? If it slipped off, it could always fly to safety.

Suddenly Frank's head appeared in the window opening. "All clear," Frank said. "Come on in."

"I don't think I can move," Joe said through clenched teeth. "Come out and get me."

"Uh, bad idea," Frank said. "Just step sideways slowly, in the direction of my voice."

Joe took a tiny step, then another.

"That's it, easy does it," Frank murmured. "You're almost there." The moment Joe was in reach, Frank wrapped his arms around his legs as Joe ducked through the window.

"I just made a change in career plans," Joe said, through lips that quivered. "I'm giving up my childhood dream of becoming a window washer!"

Half an hour later the Hardys were back at the condo, trying to make sense of what they had just learned.

"So a lot of the endorsement money is not getting to the players," Frank said. "Those two lists we saw show that it's being siphoned off, with Hyde's approval."

"That's obviously Rosen's doing," Joe said. "But then, what does he have to do with the Syndicate, and why is he so scared of it?"

Joe hesitated, then added, "There's something else that bothers me a lot more, Frank. These guys I'm playing with are such amazing athletes. Why aren't they doing better on the field? There's no way they should be losing games."

"What are you suggesting?" Frank asked.

Joe shook his head. "I don't know. After today I'm too tired to think straight. Maybe I'd better turn in."

A mischievous grin crossed Frank's face. "Are you sure you don't want to sleep outside—on the balcony?" he asked. Then he ducked, to avoid being hit by the running shoe Joe threw at him.

Joe woke up the next morning to an empty apartment. He stumbled into the kitchen, poured himself a glass of orange juice, and took it out onto the balcony, where he sat down, propped his feet on the railing, and started a mental list of his fellow Sharks. Which of them might go along with a plot to throw games, and which wouldn't?

Joe ran through the roster of forty or so players. Then he realized that he simply didn't know most of them well enough to say.

He drained his orange juice, walked back inside, and called Coach Landers's office. He told the secretary who answered the phone that he'd like to come in early to view game films with the coach, and he asked her to set it up for him.

It was nearly ten o'clock when Joe flagged a cab to the stadium. Coach Landers was waiting in his office. Joe explained what he was after.

"It's going to be hard to draw any concrete conclusions from the tapes, son," Landers said as the two of them walked down the hall to the film room. "But we can sure look."

The two of them sat down facing the screen, and Landers punched on the tape. "This is last year's game with the Toros," he said. "Watch this."

Jackson was faking a handoff to Havranek, then rolling to the right. House McMaran formed a one-man convoy for his quarterback, but instead of taking out the linebacker who was after Jackson, McMaran stumbled. The linebacker forced Jackson to hurry his pass, which fell incomplete.

"Nothing unusual there," Landers said. "Everybody misses a block now and then. But look at this."

He advanced the tape to a game with the Seattle Owls. Again McMaran missed a block at a crucial moment. And McMaran wasn't the only one. In one game after another, a linebacker fell down on pass coverage, a defensive back let a receiver slip by him, or a tight end dropped a ball he should have caught. The mistakes weren't obvious—even Coach Landers had to look closely—but they always came at crucial moments.

Finally Joe sat back. "Did you ever wonder if some of your players are trying to throw games or to shave points to beat the spread?"

"You lose often enough, and any coach starts wondering about that," Landers growled. "But no coach wants to believe it. Still . . ." His voice trailed off.

He and Joe walked back to his office. The Sharks were starting to arrive to get their injuries worked on and prepare for the afternoon's practice. Rich Havranek, a towel around his waist and thongs on his feet, passed them in the hallway. "Whatta you say, Coach, kid?" he greeted them.

"How's the hamstring?" Landers asked.

"I'm hoping the whirlpool will loosen it up," Havranek replied, making a face.

"They don't get any better than that man," Landers said to Joe as they stepped into his office. "He could have a hundred and ten-degree fever and a broken leg, and he'd figure out how to play, anyway. Too bad I don't have more like him."

Joe took a chair near Landers's desk. "Why would someone throw a game?" he demanded. "What's in it for him?"

"Money, maybe," Landers replied. "Sure, they all make a lot, but for some people, there's no such thing as enough. Or it could be some kind of blackmail."

"What happens if they're caught?" Joe asked.

Landers studied him, narrow eyed. "Son, did you ever hear of the Chicago Black Sox?" he asked. "They were a champion baseball team. Some of them agreed to throw the 1919 World Series. They were banned from pro sports for life. And that's what would happen to anyone *I* caught. We have to protect the integrity of the game."

Those words were echoing in Joe's mind a few minutes later as he stood with his foot on a bench, tying the laces of his practice shoes. Nearby, Elvin Jackson was adjusting the flak jacket he wore to protect his tender ribs.

"El?" Joe said in a quiet voice. "I hope you don't mind my asking, but I'm curious about Bobby Walker. What made him so good?"

Jackson looked over at Walker's locker, with the photographs and the uniform still hanging there. "Bobby Walker was the best," he said softly. "The best receiver I've ever seen. The best man I've ever known. He figured out the secret."

"What secret?" Joe asked.

"The secret of everything," Jackson said. "How to get the most out of life for himself and the people he cared about. You just felt better when Bobby was around."

"How did he die, El?" Joe asked softly, as he gazed at the smiling, handsome face in the photograph.

"Car accident," Jackson said. "Three years ago."

Joe decided to take a chance. "Somebody told me there was foul play involved," he said.

Jackson stared at Joe for what seemed like forever. Then he turned away and started pulling on his pads. The conversation was over.

The Sharks were getting ready to take the field when the dressing room door burst open.

In walked House McMaran, a big grin on his red face. "Okay, you turkeys, now we can play football," he roared, lifting his massive arms toward the ceiling. "The House is here."

The Sharks laughed as McMaran strode toward his locker. Some slapped him on the back as he passed. Others teased him about his antics at the Neptune Room. Joe stayed out of his way.

On the field, Joe and his fellow kick returners worked on handling squib kicks, those low line drives that are harder to deal with than a spinning top.

"Pounce on that ball like a grasshopper hops on a june bug," Coach Westcott told them. "Hug it to your chest like it was your long-lost grandma. Like this. Kick me one, Bobby Joe."

Ratliff kicked a wicked, spinning line drive. Westcott got a line on it, ran toward it at controlled speed, then suddenly turned a full somersault in midair. He hit the ground lightly, played the ball on a short hop, and neatly scooped it to his chest. Then he turned and bowed to the players, who were laughing and shaking their heads.

Waiting in line for his turn, Joe noticed Hot Rod Hill on the sidelines. He was wearing black sweats, and his ankle was in a cast. During a break Joe went over and introduced himself.

"Hey, man, I've been watching you," Hill said. "You're not after my job, are you?"

"No way," Joe said with a laugh. The idea was absurd. Hot Rod Hill had won the Heisman Trophy his senior year in college and had played in the Pro Bowl as a rookie. "I'm just keeping your spot on the bench warm."

"Well, let me know if I can help you," Hill said. "Anything you want to know, just ask."

"Well, there is one thing," Joe said, lowering his voice. "How do you keep your strength up over a long season? Can you recommend any pills, anything like that?"

Hill gave him a searching look, then said, "That's a question to ask the trainers or Doc Washington. Not me."

When practice ended, Joe went to the locker room and sat down to unlace his shoes. Somebody stopped right in back of him. He glanced up, straight into the sneering red face of House McMaran.

"You listen to me, little man," McMaran growled in a voice too low for anyone else in the room to hear. "Rookies around here keep their mouths shut. They don't ask questions. And they don't go poking into things that don't concern them. If you want to stay in one piece, you'd better remember that."

Chapter 7

Joe kept his eyes locked onto McMaran's beady, bloodshot eyes. He didn't dare let this giant bully know that he was scared. But he was—*very* scared. McMaran could injure him badly on the field any time he wanted to. What if McMaran had somehow figured out what Joe was really up to? He'd be lucky to end up with an unbroken bone in his body!

"Hey, House!" one of his lineman buddies shouted. "It's all-you-can-eat shrimp night at the Fish Factory. You coming?"

House backed away, still glaring at Joe. Joe kept his face impassive. As soon as the lineman turned away, Joe took a deep breath and let it out in a sigh of relief. He was still in one piece—so far.

When Frank picked up Joe after practice, Joe told his brother about House's threat. "It sure sounds like he's at the center of whatever's going on with the Sharks," Frank commented.

"I'll say," Joe agreed. "I'm going to do my best to stay out of his way, but it's not going to be easy."

When the Hardys got back to the condo, the light on the answering machine was blinking. Frank went over and pressed the play button.

"Don't you fellows ever stay home?" the voice of Fenton Hardy asked, chuckling. "I'm flying in tomorrow evening. My flight arrives at ten. I know it's Friday night, but please meet me at the apartment. I've uncovered some information you'll be interested in."

"Good," Frank said as the message ended. "We could use some more information around here. You know what else I need," he added. "Exercise. I know I'm on my feet all day in that stupid mailroom, but that's not enough. I need fresh air and sunshine."

"More exercise is the last thing I need," Joe said with a groan. "I'll tell you what, though. Why don't we rent bikes tomorrow morning and ride through Balboa Park? That's not far from your job. You can go straight to work afterward."

The sun was barely up when Joe and Frank rode into the park the next morning. They wore biking shorts and short-sleeved knit shirts, and the air was cool on their skin. In the early morning light, the deep green grass, rich red bougainvillea, and gray-green leaves of giant eucalyptus trees were fresh and fragrant. They rode across a graceful Roman-style bridge spanning a deep wooded canyon and coasted down a hill.

Through a gap in the trees, Frank saw the soaring blue bridge connecting San Diego to Coronado Island. He took a deep breath and felt his body come alive.

After riding around for a half an hour, they came out of the park, bought bagels and juice at a deli, and took them to a table on the sidewalk.

"So what do we know so far?" Frank asked, as he spread cream cheese on his bagel. "And where do we go from here?"

"I know one thing," Joe said. "Something weird is going on with the Sharks. Hot Rod Hill got very spooked when I asked him about pills. And Elvin Jackson wouldn't say a word when I asked about Bobby Walker's death. But I think House is the real key."

"Key to what?" Frank asked.

"He and some of his buddies are throwing games," Joe replied. "After looking at the films, I'm sure of it. Either losing or just narrowing the point spread."

Frank stroked his chin and said, "Either

way, anybody who knows about it stands to make a lot of money by betting on a sure thing."

"Somebody like Peter Hyde?" Joe asked.

"Maybe," Frank replied. "But so far we know zip about Hyde. I'm hoping Dad can fill us in on him. And about the Syndicate. I wonder what Rosen is so frightened of."

Back at the rental shop, Frank changed into his work clothes, then Joe dropped him off at the Hyde-Ruskin building. Sandy was already in the mailroom when he walked in.

"Well, Frank," she said with an impish grin, "it's been nice knowing you, but I'm moving up in the world."

"You're leaving?" Frank asked. He felt very disappointed, and that surprised him.

"Not exactly," Sandy replied. "I'm being promoted. Starting this morning, I'm going to be Andrew Rosen's assistant."

"Hey, congratulations," Frank said, patting her on the back. "So what's the next step on the ladder? Are you going to become an agent yourself someday?"

"Please don't laugh," she said, her cheeks turning pink. "But I want to be like my mother. It's that simple. I want to be a successful entrepreneur the way she is. That's why I'm studying international business at college and soaking up every bit of information I can at Hyde-Ruskin. I'm really lucky. Peter—Mr.

Hyde, I mean—promised my mom he'd do anything to help, and he has."

"Great," Frank said. "You sound really together about this, and I know you'll make it."

"Thanks." She stretched up and gave him a peck on the cheek. "But what about you, Frank? How long are you going to stay in this dead-end job?"

"It wasn't so dead-end for you," Frank replied with a grin.

Sandy's blush deepened. "That's different."

"Just kidding," Frank assured her. "As for me, who knows? Once Joe's a little more settled, I'll make up my mind if I want to stay on the West Coast or go back East. At this point, I don't know."

Frank loaded his trolley with letters and packages and started on his first round. Sandy went along—"for old times' sake," she said. She wasn't due in Rosen's office for another hour.

"So how well do you know our all-powerful boss?" Frank asked while they were alone in the elevator. "I've never even seen him."

"Peter? We're like that." Sandy held up two fingers as if they were glued together. "Well, not exactly, but he and my mother have been very close for years. When I was little, I used to come here and play in his secret passage."

"Secret passage?" Frank repeated. "Come on!"

"Well, it's really a private staircase into his office suite, but it *feels* like a secret passage. And hardly anybody knows about it."

The elevator stopped on six. Frank looked both ways, worried that Rosen might see and recognize him, but the corridor was empty.

"Here," Sandy said, picking up Rosen's packet of letters. "I might as well take these and settle into my new duties. I'll come down to say hello later."

It was just before noon when Sandy returned to the mailroom, obviously irritated. "Mr. Rosen sent me down to see if any overnight packages arrived for him," she said.

Frank double-checked his clipboard and said, "Not a thing. Sorry."

"Mr. Rosen—as that arrogant twerp told me to call him—will not be happy," Sandy said. "Actually, he's already unhappy, not to say scared out of his wits."

"About what?" Frank asked, trying to keep his interest from showing too plainly.

Sandy shrugged. "Beats me. He got a phone call from somebody while he was showing me his file system. He was so nervous that I think he forgot I was in the room. Can you believe he made a date to meet this guy at Camel Rock at ten o'clock at night? Freaky."

Frank raised his eyebrows and asked, "Where's Camel Rock? In Saudi Arabia?"

"No, silly, it's up the coast, in Torrey Pines

State Park." Sandy gave him a mischievous grin. "Near the hang glider port. You remember the hang glider port, don't you?"

"I'll never forget," Frank said wryly.

A delivery man walked through the door with a stack of packages. Frank signed for them, then glanced through the stack. "Nothing for your boss," he told Sandy.

"Well, that's that," she said. "I'd better go break the bad news to *Mr.* Rosen. The creep!"

After leaving the stadium, Joe got stuck in a traffic jam. It was close to six by the time he reached the Hyde-Ruskin building. Frank was waiting on the sidewalk in front of the building.

"I was getting worried," Frank said, as he settled into the passenger seat. "We have to be somewhere at ten."

"I know," Joe replied. "That's when Dad's plane comes in. But he doesn't expect us to meet him at the airport. We can go out and eat and still be back in plenty of time."

"Change of plans," Frank said. "We're going on a hike tonight at ten."

"A hike?" Joe said. He glanced over at Frank to see if he was kidding. "Don't you think you're taking this exercise stuff a little far?"

"Listen to this." Frank repeated what Sandy had overheard.

Joe tapped the wheel with his fist. "Yes!" he exclaimed. "Now we're getting somewhere. A mysterious meeting in the dead of night! You know what, Frank? If I were Rosen, I'd think very seriously about leaving town instead of showing up."

Frank and Joe left the condo just after nine and drove north on the Coast Highway. Past the university, the highway dipped into a valley that opened onto the ocean. Even by night it was breathtakingly beautiful.

A little farther up the highway, Frank spotted a rustic sign for Torrey Pines State Park. He turned off onto the access road, then hit the brakes. There was a heavy iron gate across the road. He got out and checked it out, then came back, shaking his head.

"It's locked," he reported. "And I don't think I can pick it. We'll have to walk up."

"I *knew* you were going to trick me into a hike." Joe let out an exaggerated groan.

They parked the car in a secluded spot, climbed over the fence, and started up the steep, winding road. By the time they reached the adobe park headquarters building, they were both breathing hard.

"What time is it?" Joe asked.

Frank pushed the little button that lit up his watch. "Ten minutes to ten," he said. "Where do you suppose Camel Rock is?"

"There's a trail map on that rack," Joe replied. He pulled a tiny flashlight from his pocket and studied the map, then said, "To the left, one and a quarter miles. We'd better hurry."

The trail took them high above the ocean. In the moonlight it was spooky. Eerie sandstone formations jutted up here and there, and the majestic Torrey pines cast long, inky black shadows. The waist-high sagebrush filled the air with a clean, bracing fragrance. Overhead, millions of stars glimmered in the dark blue sky. The only sounds were the rustle of their footsteps and the far-off crash of the surf below them.

They saw Camel Rock long before they got there. It was the largest, most prominent rock formation in the park. As they approached it, Frank touched Joe's arm and gestured that they should get off the winding trail and into the sagebrush. Walking silently, they crossed a service road coming from the other direction and stopped under a tall, isolated pine to listen.

Still the only sound was the lapping of waves at the bottom of the cliff.

"What now?" Joe whispered.

"Let's go to the end of the trail," Frank replied.

Frank's eyes were completely adjusted to the dark. Ahead, he could see the edge of the cliff and make out a line of whitecaps far below. There was a clearing at the trail's end, but it was empty. Frank pressed the button that lit his watch dial again—it said ten-twenty.

"Maybe they've already come and gone," Joe whispered. "Should we backtrack?"

"I guess so," Frank murmured, disappointed. "Wait! Joe, look at the edge of the cliff. That bench. It's smashed!"

Joe made a disgusted noise. "Vandals. Even in a beautiful place like this they wreck things."

"Not so fast," Frank said. "The railing at the edge of the cliff is smashed, too. Come on!"

Frank scanned the clearing again, then hurried across to the edge, with Joe right behind him. Together, they peered over the cliff.

Suddenly Joe clutched Frank's arm. "There," he exclaimed, pointing with his other hand. "On the rocks near the bottom—it's a car!"

It looked like a smashed-in can.

"I have a horrible feeling," Frank said. "What if it belonged to Rosen?"

Joe nodded grimly. "Yeah—and what if Rosen was in it!"

Chapter 8

FRANK STARED at the crumpled car on the rocks below. "I don't see how we can climb down there to check if anyone's inside," he said. "We'd better find a phone and notify the authorities."

They started back on the path, walking quickly. As they were recrossing the service road, Joe suddenly stopped. "Wait," he said. "What was that?"

Frank held his breath and listened. From a clump of sagebrush to the left of the path came rustling and a faint groan.

"Over there," Frank said softly. "It sounds like someone's hurt."

Joe took out his flashlight and shone the beam on the sagebrush. From under the foliage, a pair of legs protruded. One of them twitched.

Frank and Joe rushed over and dropped to their knees. "It's Andy Rosen," Frank said, as the flashlight revealed a bloodied face.

Rosen opened his eyes, then turned his head to avoid the glare of the light.

"What happened?" Frank demanded. "Can you move?"

"It hurts," he whimpered. "All over."

"Can you sit up?" Joe asked. "Do you want to stay here while we go for help?"

"No!" Rosen pushed himself to a sitting position. "Don't tell anyone. They'll kill me if you do!"

Rosen was a mess. His expensive blue pinstriped suit was ripped and dirty, and his fancy tasseled loafers were badly scuffed. He looked at Frank and his eyes widened. "You," he said, in a baffled voice. "What are you doing here? I don't get it. Aren't you with the Syndicate?"

Frank made a lightning-quick decision. It was time to tell Rosen the truth—or part of it, at least.

"No," he said, "I'm not. In fact, I'm trying to find out exactly what the Syndicate is."

"I'm afraid I can't tell you much about it," Rosen said, "except that Peter Hyde is involved in it."

Joe said, "Is that what happened to you? You tangled with the Syndicate?"

Rosen shook his head, then looked as if he wished he hadn't. "I'm a gambler," he said. "A rotten gambler. I thought I could get out of the hole I was in by betting a lot of money I didn't have on the Sharks' winning against Atlanta. But they lost. So there I was in a deeper hole. The guys I owe the money to have their own ways of collecting."

"What about skimming the Sharks' endorsement contracts?" Frank asked. "Didn't you make enough off that to set you straight?"

Rosen acted surprised. "If you're not with the Syndicate, how do you know about that?" he asked.

"We have our ways," Frank said.

"I do the skimming for Peter Hyde," Rosen explained. "He knows about my gambling habit, so I have no choice. I wanted to stop, and even told Hyde so last week, but he wouldn't hear of it."

Frank whistled low. "Don't you think that might explain what happened here?"

Rosen's frightened eyes grew wide. "You mean the Syndicate, not the people I owe money to, had me beaten up?"

Frank nodded.

"Exactly what did happen here?" Joe asked.

"I drove up from the other side of the park and left my car on the service road," Rosen said. "Then I waited for dark and walked to Camel Rock. Two guys grabbed me. They both had guns. One of them kept me covered while the other one beat me up. They said this was my last warning. That's all I remember."

"You'd better come with us," Frank said.

"No, thanks," Rosen replied. "Just help me to my car. I'll make it back all right."

Joe cleared his throat. "It's not that simple," he said. "Your car—"

Rosen jerked his head up. "What about it? Where's my car?" he demanded, his voice rising.

"At the bottom of the cliff," Frank told him. "Those gorillas must have pushed it over."

"Oh, no! What am I going to do now?" Rosen said.

"We'll drive you home," Joe offered. "But if I were you, I'd think about visiting some friend who lives out of town."

"Yeah—maybe my brother in Seattle," Rosen said. "I haven't seen him in a while. But it's important to keep up with family, right?"

Frank snorted. "Sure—especially when you're in trouble. Come on, we'll help you to our car."

The hike to the foot of the hill took a long time. Joe squeezed into the backseat of the convertible while Frank helped Rosen into the passenger seat. He was silent on the drive into town, as if he was just beginning to realize the mess he had gotten himself into. When Frank pulled up in front of his seafront apartment building, he blinked and said, "Thanks, guys."

"One more thing," Frank said. "The other day, you were talking on the phone about somebody named Hardy. What was that about?"

"Hardy?" Rosen shrugged, then winced with pain. "Oh, yes. Hardy's a new guy on the Sharks. I was talking to Melissa Sharpe about whether to sign him. She said to wait until Hardy had talked to Jennifer Washington."

Joe frowned. Rosen obviously didn't know who he was. "Why?" he demanded.

Rosen said, "Beats me."

"Is she part of the Syndicate?" Joe pressed.

Rosen's eyes narrowed. "I've always assumed so."

Frank and Joe remained silent, taking in the information. At last Frank handed Rosen a scrap of paper and a pen and told him to write down his brother's phone number in Seattle.

After Rosen had done so, he opened the door and pushed himself to his feet. Staggering a little, he walked to the glass door of the building and disappeared inside.

Joe climbed into the passenger seat and focused straight ahead. "Home, James," he said with a quick salute of his right hand.

When Frank and Joe entered the apartment, they found their father in his shirtsleeves and a loosened tie, sitting at the dining room table, thumbing through a stack of computer printouts.

He looked up with a big smile. "I was wondering where you were," he said. "Are you all right?"

"We're fine, Dad," Frank answered. "But it's been hectic."

"Maybe we should fill you in," Joe added, pulling out another of the dining room chairs and sitting down.

After Frank and Joe had told their father everything, Fenton Hardy leaned back in his chair.

"I'm sure this thing is bigger than Rosen skimming money, Dad," Frank concluded. "It's even bigger than some of the Sharks shaving points."

"And it sounds as if both Melissa Sharpe and Peter Hyde are major players," Joe added.

Fenton nodded. "I suspect you're right," he said. "You've done well, both of you."

"How about you, Dad?" Joe asked. "What did you discover?"

Fenton tapped the printouts on the table. "I found a paper trail that leads in some very intriguing directions," he said. "This is in strict confidence. For now, I don't mean to share it even with Nicky Chambers. We're dealing with a complex web, and at this point I'm not sure who might be caught up in it."

"That sounds like the Syndicate," Frank said.

"I knew the name Peter Hyde rang a bell," Fenton continued. "But it was only after I talked to my friends at Interpol that I remembered why. About ten years ago Hyde's partner, a man named Walter Ruskin, was lost at sea. He was on Hyde's yacht at the time, and he simply disappeared. Hyde told investigators that he thought his partner went for a walk on deck late at night, suffered a heart attack, and fell overboard."

"Did the authorities buy his story?" Joe asked. "It sounds sort of fishy to me."

"It did to them as well," Fenton replied, "especially when they discovered that Hyde stood to profit handsomely from his partner's death. But they couldn't find a shred of evidence to prove that Hyde was responsible for Ruskin's death."

"Who else was aboard?" Joe asked.

"Hyde, and the crew, of course," Fenton replied. "And Melissa Sharpe."

Joe heard Frank gasp. He glanced at his older brother and then at his father.

Fenton stared at Frank, who was focusing on his clasped hands. "From what you've told me, it sounds as if you and Sandy Sharpe have become close friends."

Frank sighed, then nodded.

"I wonder if this relationship is wise, Frank," Fenton said. "It could lead to trouble."

Frank remained silent for a moment. At last he said, "I'll be truthful with you, Dad. I like Sandy a lot, and I've come close to telling her what we're doing. I haven't yet. But even though Melissa's her mother, I think Sandy can help us if we bring her into the investigation. Maybe Hyde's forcing Melissa Sharpe to do things she doesn't want to. . . ." His words trailed off.

"And you, Joe? What do you think?" Fenton asked.

"Frank's probably right," Joe replied after a short hesitation.

Fenton tapped his fingertips on the table, then said, "I trust your judgment. But remember, we're dealing with cold-blooded professionals. They'll stop at nothing."

"I'll remember," Frank said. "I'll call Sandy first thing in the morning."

Sandy sounded out of breath when she answered the phone Saturday morning. "Frank! I'm glad you caught me," she said. "I was almost out the door. I'm going out for a spin in our boat."

"Can we meet later today?" Frank asked.

"I'll tell you what," Sandy replied. "There's a seafood restaurant up the coast at Del Mar that does a terrific weekend brunch. I'll go up by boat and meet you there at eleven."

Frank found the place easily. He was sitting

at a table on the rooftop terrace, enjoying the sunshine, when he saw Sandy walking up the hill from the pier. He watched appreciatively. She was wearing white shorts over a hot pink swimsuit, with a white sweater tied loosely around her neck, and her long, blond hair gleamed in the sun.

"How was the boat ride?" he asked as she joined him at the table.

"Great," she said, giving him a hug. Frank ordered her a glass of fresh orange juice, and when it came, they toasted the weekend.

"So, what prompted you to call?" Sandy asked merrily. "I hope you aren't going to ask me to marry you. We're both too young, and I just couldn't tie myself down to a mailroom clerk. Don't be offended, but you don't make enough to support the ten kids I'm planning to have."

Frank grinned. "Nope, no proposals today," he said, and felt a little guilty about his girl friend, Callie Shaw. He waited until after they had ordered breakfast, then began to tell her who he really was and why he and Joe were in San Diego. As he talked, her eyes grew wider.

"I *knew* it," she said when he finished. "I knew you didn't belong in a mailroom. And that brother of yours asks too many questions to be a simple jock with nothing on his mind but his career. Okay, what next?"

Frank hesitated. "We've got a lot of pieces

of the puzzle," he said. "Steroids, high-stakes gambling, Bobby Walker's death, your new boss—but it isn't clear how they fit together. There's something else. It looks to me as if Peter Hyde may be right in the middle of this."

At the mention of Hyde's name, Sandy's smile faded. "Frank—do you know something you're not telling me? Something about my mother?"

Frank didn't want to lie, but he wasn't ready to share what his father had found out about the death of Walter Ruskin and the possible involvement of Melissa Sharpe. Before he could decide what to do, Sandy spoke again.

"I need to know the truth, Frank. Peter Hyde has always been good to me, but I've never been convinced that he has my mother's best interests at heart. I'm willing to take this wherever it leads. I think we ought to take a look at Peter's office. It's Saturday, and no one will be there."

Frank hesitated. "How do we get in?"

"I have a key," Sandy replied. "Peter gave it to me years ago. We can take your car. The boat'll be fine where it is."

At that point, the waiter approached with their brunch. "First, we eat," Frank told her. "Never do detective work on an empty stomach."

They left Frank's car a block away from Hyde-Ruskin and walked in the front door of the building. Sandy signed them in. The guard seemed to know her. Upstairs, Frank followed her past a row of offices on the sixth floor to an unmarked door that looked as if it led to a cleaning closet. Sandy inserted her key in the lock and pulled the door open. Behind it, Frank saw a spiral staircase.

Sandy grinned and gestured for Frank to go first. At the top of the stairs another door led to Hyde's private penthouse office. Frank stepped inside and gave a low whistle. It was like a velvet cave. The walls and ceiling were black, as was the thick carpeting. Hyde's desk was a massive piece of jagged black marble resting on two squat columns cut from black stone.

On one wall was a huge TV screen. Set into another wall was a bank of smaller monitors showing changing views of the Hyde-Ruskin offices.

"Trusting fellow," Frank joked. Then he noticed a flickering light on Hyde's computer. He had left it on!

Frank sat down and started scrolling through the files, not noticing anything that was obviously incriminating. All at once he stopped.

Sandy hurried over.

The file, called *Victory,* listed selected Sharks games over the past five seasons, with the pregame point spreads and final scores. The Sharks had won some and lost others, but in each case, they never beat the spread. Anybody who had bet against them would have cleaned up. The upcoming Toro game was listed, too, with the point spread. The Sharks were favored to win by seven.

"See that?" Frank said. "Even if the Sharks win, if it's by less than seven points, the people who bet on the Toros collect. And if you *know* they'll win by less than seven, you can make a fortune." Frank closed the file.

"Try that one," Sandy suggested, pointing to a file called *Jackpot.*

In it was a tally of money owed to Peter Hyde—adding up to millions. Frank whistled. "This guy doesn't play penny ante, does he?" he exclaimed, cutting off when he heard voices in the outer office.

"Quick," he whispered, hitting the keys that closed the file and darkened the screen. He and Sandy hurried to the door that led to the spiral staircase. Just as they closed the door behind them, they heard the other door open.

"We'll move as soon as the Toros humiliate Nicky's boys on Sunday," a man's voice said.

"That's Peter," Sandy whispered to Frank.

"Is the money in place?" a woman asked.

Frank heard Sandy gasp. Her mother was in the office with Hyde.

"McMaran says we're set for Sunday," Hyde continued, "but he's such an oaf, I can never be sure. He's our weakest link. We'll have to take care of him after the game. And that new guy, too. Doc Washington tells me he didn't want to take his pills and that he's asking too many questions."

"Please," Melissa said, "don't hurt him. He's just a kid."

"A kid who's too smart for his own good," Hyde returned. "He has to learn to mind his own business—the hard way if necessary."

Frank had heard enough. He touched Sandy's shoulder and pointed down the spiral stairs. As he turned, his foot slipped on the edge of a step. He frantically grabbed for the railing, but missed. As he slid down the stairs, first on his bottom and then on his back, it sounded like a herd of kids racing out to recess. He lay stunned, unable to catch his breath at the foot of the stairs. He knew he was just about to meet Peter Hyde, face-to-face.

Chapter 9

FRANK WAS STILL LYING there catching his breath when Sandy grabbed him, opened the door at the bottom of the stairs, propped it open, and helped him out into the hallway—all before Peter Hyde opened the door at the top of the stairs.

"Stay here. I'll stall them," she whispered, giving him a quick pat on the shoulder.

She took a deep breath, squared her shoulders, and reopened the door. A moment later Frank heard her say, "Oh, Peter, Mom, hi, you're here. Good, I don't have to leave you a message. I came in this morning to make sure I was up to speed in my new job with Andy Rosen. I'd just hate to be unprepared. Anyway, the thing is, I want to take the boat out this afternoon. You're not planning to use it, are you? I mean, if you are, it's okay. I'll make other plans."

"We're going out on my boat," Hyde replied. "Was that you out here just now? It sounded like a herd of buffalo on the stairs."

Sandy gave a perfect imitation of an embarrassed laugh. "I'm afraid so," she said. "The thing is, I started up the stairs, and then I remembered I had a report for you from Mr. Rosen's office, but I'd forgotten it. And when I turned to go back down, I fell."

"Are you all right, dear?" Sandy's mother asked. "Did you hurt yourself?"

"Just my pride," Sandy said. "You two are going to have a great day on the water. It's really nice out. Oh, are you coming down this way?"

Frank struggled to his feet and hobbled down the corridor while Sandy continued to chat with her mother. Just as the doorknob turned, he found an unlocked janitor's closet and ducked inside. His ankle felt strained and his back hurt, but nothing seemed to be broken. From the dark interior of the closet, he heard Sandy, her mother, and Peter Hyde walk down the hall to the elevator.

A few minutes later he heard the elevator return. "Frank?" Sandy called. "Frank, where are you? Come on out, it's okay."

Frank opened the closet door and stepped

into the hallway. Sandy was standing there, head down, fists clenched, tears running down her cheeks. Frank limped over to her and put his arm around her shoulders.

"I'm so ashamed," she whispered to him. "Ashamed, and terribly afraid."

Joe woke up late. He pulled on a T-shirt and running shorts and joined his father, who was enjoying coffee and the morning paper on the balcony.

"What time do you have to be down at the stadium today?" Fenton asked.

"We have a light workout at noon," Joe said, yawning and stretching his arms toward the sky. "I was thinking about going down early, because I figure I'll be as jumpy as a jack rabbit. The closer I get to tomorrow's game, the harder it is for me to keep still."

"Why don't I drive you?" Fenton said. "I'd like a chance to sit down with Nicky Chambers and go over what we know up to this point."

Fenton called ahead to the Sharks' owner to tell him the two of them were coming. As they headed along the Coast Highway toward town, Joe noticed what a beautiful day it was. Kites were flying in Mission Bay Park. Sailboats skated across the bay. Joe glanced at his father, who had insisted on driving. His left arm rested on the door frame, and he had the hint of a smile on his face.

"You look pretty cool in a sports car," Joe said with a laugh. "I wish Mom could see you."

Fenton smiled. "She'd probably tell me to act my age," he said.

At the stadium Nicky Chambers was waiting for them in his office. He was standing before the aquarium, watching TD the shark's graceful loops and dives.

"I wonder what it would be like," he mused, "to know that you're the most powerful creature in your environment, that no enemy can hope to prevail against you?"

"Fishermen catch sharks," Fenton pointed out. "And sharks occasionally kill men. Nothing's simple—including this case you handed us."

"I want to hear all about it," Chambers said. "But first, how are you? And you, Joe—is Deke treating you all right?"

Joe groaned and then laughed. "Well, he doesn't play favorites," he said. "He treats us all like dogs. No, seriously, sir, he's a fine coach."

"I know that," Chambers said. "And he deserves a better reward for his efforts than he's been getting lately."

Chambers motioned them to the long couch in the corner of the office, then moved a chair to face them. "Well?" he demanded. "What's the verdict?"

"It's much too soon to be talking about verdicts," Fenton replied. "What we can give you at this point is an assessment of the situation and some suspicions. Getting the evidence to back them up is the next step. Joe, why don't you tell Nicky what you've learned so far?"

Chambers's face darkened as Joe told of his run-ins with House McMaran, his troubling conversations with Doc Washington, and his reasons for suspecting that some of the players were throwing games. The older man gripped the arms of his chair, then let his shoulders slump forward.

"And you, Fenton?" Nicky asked when Joe reached the end of his report.

"It's not good, Nicky," Fenton Hardy said. "In Vegas the word is that there's an unusual amount of action against the Sharks on Sunday. I suspect that's largely Hyde at work—or him and his high-roller friends. And they wouldn't bet the ranch if they didn't have good reason to think a fix was on."

The tiredness seemed to leave Chambers's face. "Say the Sharks win, as they ought to, and beat the point spread," he said softly. "What will that mean to Hyde and his jackal friends?"

Fenton smiled grimly. "At best, they'll be cleaned out," he replied. "And if, as I suspect, they're laying much bigger bets than they can actually cover if they lose, they could find themselves in a very bad spot."

Chambers focused on the aquarium as TD swam into view. It seemed to Joe that he was carrying on a silent conversation with the shark. "Then that's our answer," he said. "Hyde may think he's all-powerful, but he doesn't know who he's dealing with this time," he added cryptically.

Joe and Fenton stood up to leave. Nicky walked them to the door, his arms around their shoulders. "So, Joe," he said, his normal good humor returning, "I hear you've been wowing them on the practice field. Is that true?"

"I hope so," Joe said. "As far as I'm concerned, Coach can drop that fair-catch restriction right now. A little hint from the team owner ought to help."

Nicky laughed and clapped Joe on the back. "Sorry, son," he said. "This owner never interferes with on-field operations." He looked at Fenton. "How much longer, do you think?"

Fenton paused at the door. "We're getting close, Nicky," he replied. "But as I said, what we need now is proof. And don't forget, our opponents are smart. They must be sensing that someone's onto them, and they won't sit still for that. They'll react."

"Do you have another minute, Fenton?" Chambers asked. "I just thought of a few more details. Joe, you go ahead. We don't want Coach fining you for being late."

As Joe stood in the elevator taking him

down to the dressing room, he realized how frustrated he was by what Nicky had said about the fair-catch rule. His father, he knew, was relieved. He was trying to think of some way to get Coach Landers to change his mind when the elevator stopped at the upper-deck level. The doors slid opened, and House McMaran got on.

"Well, well," McMaran said. "Just the little shrimp I was looking for." He crowded Joe into the far corner of the elevator. Joe reached for the control panel, but House effortlessly pushed his arm back down.

"What's the matter, House?" Joe asked, acting as baffled and innocent as he could.

"You are, little man," McMaran growled as the elevator took them to the basement level. "Butting into things that are none of your business. Just make sure you don't get in the way of what's going on. You might live to regret it—or you might not."

The elevator door opened. McMaran grabbed Joe by the arm and pulled him into the hallway. He had a big grin on his face, as if he and Joe had just been involved in some friendly roughhousing.

Joe pulled away, and McMaran gave him another ugly look before entering the dressing room. Joe waited a moment then walked in by himself. He quickly put on his uniform. "Full pads," said a note on the chalkboard. Everybody was grumbling about that.

Saturdays were normally easy days—but not this one. Joe didn't know if Coach Landers was trying to shake things up or if he was still steamed about the loss to Atlanta. Whatever the reason, he was pushing the team mercilessly.

After an hour of stretches and sprints, Landers called for kicking practice.

Westcott tossed Joe a red mesh vest, the signal to the rest of the team that the wearer was not to be tackled. "Here, put this on. I can't afford to lose another guy," he said, jerking his thumb toward a forlorn Hot Rod Hill, watching from the sideline.

And then the practice runbacks began—to the right, to the left, up the center, over and over again. They even practiced a reverse that Westcott wanted to use if they got desperate on Sunday. Old Crazy Legs loved trick plays.

"Get to the wall!" Westcott shouted as Joe gathered in another punt and raced toward the right sideline.

"Why does he keep saying that?" Joe muttered, watching his blockers set up and start searching for someone to hit. He must have fielded ten punts already, and he was ready to drop. "I'm *getting* to the wall," he said through clenched teeth.

Joe's legs felt like rubber, and he could tell the whole team felt the same way. He could hear the guys complaining as they lumbered slowly back upfield.

"Okay, one more time, and we'll call it quits," Landers called. "*If* we do it right."

Once more, Joe lined up near the goal line. Once more he watched Bobby Joe Ratliff swing his long leg into the ball. "Leroy!" he heard his upback shout, meaning that his blocking wall was setting up to the left. Joe fielded the ball cleanly, tucked it against his side, and sprinted to his left. He got beyond his wall of blockers and turned upfield.

Suddenly something hit him—something that felt like a speeding truck. One of the linemen coming downfield had ignored the red jersey and bashed into Joe while running full speed, driving him back and into a bench on the sidelines. But Joe never saw what hit him.

He lay on the turf, unable to move, hardly able to breathe. Was his back broken? Would he ever walk? He tried to open his eyes.

House McMaran had one knee on Joe's chest. He bent closer and growled, "Welcome to the pros, little buddy. You're playing with the big boys now."

"Get off him!" Joe heard Coach Westcott shout. "Get out of the way! Trainer, call an ambulance!"

Those were the last words Joe remembered.

Chapter 10

JOE TRIED TO OPEN his eyes, but the light overhead was much too bright. He narrowed his eyes to slits and tried to turn his head to see where he was. The movement made his neck hurt. He settled back against a pillow.

"He's awake, Dad," he heard a voice say, and slowly turned his head toward the voice. Frank was standing there. Behind him a white curtain hung, creating a private space around Joe's bed. This must be a hospital, he decided.

Joe touched his thigh with one hand. He was still in uniform.

"Anybody get the license number on that truck?" Joe whispered. He tried to laugh, but it came out as a groan. He shifted his gaze and saw his father standing on the other side of the bed.

"It was no truck," Fenton Hardy said. "From what I hear, it was a house—House McMaran. How do you feel, son?"

"I ache in a hundred different places, and my neck hurts, but otherwise I'm fine," Joe said. "Where am I?" he asked.

"You're in the emergency room of a hospital," Frank said. "You've been unconscious for twenty minutes or more."

Joe tried to concentrate. "It was McMaran who hit me? Why did he do it?" he asked.

"Who knows why he does anything?" Frank answered angrily. "He was on steroids. He was tired. He was angry at having to work so hard. And maybe he suspects that you're closing in on his little arrangement with Hyde—whatever it is. He wants you out of the picture."

"I just remembered, he warned me," Joe said, trying to sit up, but falling back. "This morning in the elevator after I left you and Mr. Chambers, Dad. He told me not to get in the way or I'd be sorry."

"I should never have let you go through with this," Fenton said. "But at least it's over as far as you're concerned."

"What do you mean it's over?" Joe asked, defiance in his voice.

"It's okay," Frank said. "We're beginning to get a picture of what's going on. You don't have to stay with the Sharks. What we have to do now—search for evidence—we can do from the outside to get the goods on the key players. Dad is worried about your getting badly hurt. So am I."

"It's not over till it's over," Joe said. He sat up. Swiveling, he put his feet on the floor and peeked under the bed for his shoes. "I'm going back. McMaran isn't going to win that easily."

"I'm not just talking about you, Joe," Fenton said. "I want both of you off the case and back home in Bayport. After what Frank told me he discovered on Hyde's computer this morning, I realize that this is simply too dangerous for the two of you to be involved in."

Now it was Frank's turn to argue. "But, Dad," he said, "we're getting so close! Haven't you always taught us that you can't quit when the going gets tough? You can't pull us off the case just when it gets interesting."

"I should have known my words would come back to haunt me," Fenton muttered.

A young doctor in light green scrubs pulled the curtain back, interrupting the discussion. "Up and around, huh? How do you feel, sport?" he asked Joe.

"I feel fine," Joe replied. "Never better."

"Let me look in your eyes," the doctor said. He shone a small, pinpoint light into Joe's eyes, then had him track the light with his eyes from left to right. "How's the headache?" he asked.

"It's gone," Joe said. "I tell you I'm fine."

"Well, you're free to go," the doctor said, "although I'd take it easy for a while. You might need a couple of aspirins tonight. And good luck against L.A. tomorrow," he added, shaking Joe's hand.

"There! See, Dad? I'm fine," Joe said, a gleam in his eyes. "Come on. You've got to let us finish what we started."

Fenton looked at Joe and then at Frank. "It's against my better judgment," he said, "but all right. You can stay on the case."

Frank grabbed his father's hand and shook it vigorously. Joe gave him a quick hug. "Now get me back to the stadium," he said, almost running down the hallway of the emergency room. "We're going to show House that you can't keep a good man down—especially not a Hardy."

The Sharks were still on the field when Joe got back. Coach Landers, standing atop his coach's tower, saw him emerge from the tunnel and called a break.

Joe's teammates gathered around, welcoming him back with high fives and hugs.

Joe tensed up as House McMaran ambled over. There was a TV crew on the sidelines, filming the scene for the evening newscasts. The giant lineman stuck out his big paw and said, "Sorry, little buddy. Sometimes I get carried away."

McMaran had a different message when the

Sharks took a water break half an hour later, though. Slurping water from a plastic bottle, he sidled up to Joe. "I hope you got the message, shrimp," he growled. "Whatever you're up to, back off or you'll get it a hundred times worse."

He tossed the empty bottle at Joe's feet and stomped away. Joe glanced around. This time, the cameras were nowhere in sight.

The long, tedious practice came to a merciful end at five o'clock. Coach Landers walked up the runway with Joe. "You think you'll be ready, son?" he asked. "If you don't feel like you're a hundred percent, we can go with Havranek as deep man on Sunday. It's spreading him a little thin, but he's done it before."

"The doctor says I'm ready, Coach," Joe said. "And I say so, too. I'll be there."

Jennifer Washington was waiting for Joe in the hallway outside the locker room. "How are you feeling?" she asked worriedly.

"I'm all right," Joe said. "My head hurts a little, and my ribs ache, but I'll be okay." He was tired of answering the same question.

"Did the doctor in ER give you his okay?" Washington asked.

"Sure did," Joe said. "And he wished me luck tomorrow."

"That's fine then. Can you come by the office on your way out?" Washington asked.

Joe took a long, hot shower, changed into

his street clothes, then tapped on Washington's door.

"Come in and sit down," the conditioning coach said. "I want to ask you about your training regimen. Are you sticking to it?"

"Pretty closely," Joe answered.

"You don't seem to have gained weight this week. Are you taking your tablets?"

"Well—sometimes I forget," Joe mumbled.

Washington narrowed her eyes at Joe. "Forget?" she repeated.

"Yeah, I don't know. It's been crazy," Joe told her. "Why are they so important?"

"They're important because I told you to take them, young man," Washington said, obviously keeping her temper under control. "You need to learn that you have to do what the doctor orders."

Joe shrugged his shoulders, left Washington's office, and walked outside. Frank was waiting in the car.

"Weird," Joe said, settling into the passenger seat and buckling his seat belt. He recounted his conversation with Washington.

"It sounds to me as if she's trying to get you on steroids, along with McMaran and who knows how many other guys on the team," Frank said. "Of course, I could be wrong. Maybe she's just interested in your health. Which reminds me, how's your head?"

"It hurts," Joe said, "but don't tell Dad. It's not that bad."

"Maybe a pizza would help," Frank said. "Sandy showed me a good, old-fashioned family-run place over in Little Italy. You up for it?"

"Sure," Joe said, his mind on House McMaran. He told Frank what House had said toward the end of practice.

"I think what he means," Frank commented as he pulled into the restaurant parking lot, "is that the fix is in for tomorrow's game. If you're not going to help, he wants to make sure you don't get in the way."

"At least we've got some good men on our side," Joe mused. "Jackson, Havranek—I can think of a dozen others who look like they hate what's happening to the Sharks as much as we do."

After they finished their pizza, Frank took the wheel again and headed up the Coast Highway. He was beginning to feel comfortable after driving the same stretch of road so many times. Then he glanced in his mirror and noticed headlights moving up on him fast. The car flashed its high beams, and Frank moved into the right lane to let it pass. But the car stayed behind him, closer now, and flashed its lights again.

"Hang on, Joe," Frank muttered. "No way

am I stopping, not after what happened to Rosen."

He crammed the gearshift into second and floored the accelerator. The sixteen-valve dual-overhead cam engine screamed as the tachometer needle climbed into the red zone past 7500 rpm. After making a lightning shift into third, Frank felt the forward motion of the convertible press him back into the contoured bucket seat. The little sports car was fast, no question about it.

But a glance in the mirror showed that the car behind them was just as fast, or maybe even faster. It was pulling out to pass now, and Frank could see that it was a powerful European sports sedan, more than a match for his light convertible. As they entered a lonely stretch of highway running beside the sea, the other car moved closer, forcing Frank toward the gravel shoulder.

Frank hit the brakes hard, the wheels skidding to a stop. The other car angled in just in front of him and squealed to a stop. The doors flew open, and two men jumped out. Frank had just enough time to recognize Joe's teammates Elvin Jackson and Rich Havranek. Then he saw that Jackson had a revolver in his hand. He was pointing it straight at Frank.

Chapter 11

Elvin Jackson raced to the driver's side of the car, Havranek to the passenger's side. Before Joe and Frank had time to protest, the two Sharks jerked them out of their seats and pushed them up against the car.

Jackson took one step back and pointed the revolver at Frank's stomach. Frank could easily have disarmed him—he knew at least three different techniques for taking a gun from someone who was careless or inexperienced enough to come within reach. He restrained himself from using any of them until he had a better fix on the situation. The way the gun barrel was trembling told him that Jackson was more scared than he was, and Frank knew that nothing is more dangerous than a nervous amateur with a gun.

"Take it easy, friend," Frank murmured in a soothing voice. He raised his hands to shoulder height and stood balanced on both feet, ready to react.

Joe was simply trying to breathe. After pulling him from the car, Havranek had dragged him around to Frank's side, then straightened him with a withering forearm shiver. This was the blocking-back technique he used on defensive linemen who thought they could sack the Sharks quarterback. He pressed his powerful forearm into Joe's neck, cutting off the air.

"Okay, Hardy," the halfback growled. "I don't want to hurt you, but your little game has gone on long enough."

"What game?" Joe gasped. "What are you talking about?"

"You know exactly what we're talking about," Havranek replied, pushing his face to within inches of Joe's. "We've seen you snooping around, asking questions. This team has enough problems without another one of Hyde's stooges coming in and wrecking what's left."

Jackson glanced down at the gun as if surprised to find it in his fist. He shifted his aim to point it at the ground, but he still kept staring at Frank. "Come on, admit it," he demanded. "You work for Hyde. We know you do. Well, we want you two out of here in the next twenty-four hours."

"I work for Hyde's company, sure," Frank replied. "In the mailroom. What of it?"

"We've had it with Hyde's schemes," Havranek told him. "We're going to beat him any way we can, even if people get hurt."

Frank's head was spinning. Were the two Sharks sincere? Or were they actually in league with Hyde and attempting a double fake? The only way to find out was to come clean.

"I don't want anybody to get hurt, either," he told Jackson and Havranek. "But the best way to beat Hyde is to find out what he's up to. That's what we're trying to do."

"Not according to Doc Washington," Jackson said. "She told me she has proof that both of you work for Hyde."

"And you believed that pill-pusher? Come off it," Joe said.

"You leave Doc out of it!" Jackson shouted angrily, raising the pistol until it pointed at Joe.

Frank had had enough of this one-sided discussion. He shifted his weight to his right foot and lashed out, striking the quarterback's wrist with his left heel. The pistol sailed in a graceful arc that ended in a bush nearby. Before Jackson could recover, Frank was behind him with an elbow clamped around his throat and a knee pressed into his kidney.

While Frank overpowered Jackson, Joe could see Havranek's attention slip. Seizing his chance, Joe scrambled beside Frank, facing

Havranek. He was balanced lightly on both feet, his loosely clasped fists raised in a guarding position that could shift to offense in a flash.

"We don't want to fight with you guys," Frank said quickly before Havranek could decide to attack. "Not if you're against what Hyde is doing to the Sharks."

"We should work together," Joe added.

Jackson struggled to break free, but Frank tightened his hold.

"Let him go," Havranek growled. "If you're not Hyde's thugs, who are you?"

"I'll be glad to let him go if you promise to be sensible," Frank told him. "Will you?"

"Yeah," Havranek said. Jackson managed to nod his head, signaling that he agreed as well.

Frank released his choke hold and jumped back a couple of feet, ready for anything. But the Sharks quarterback simply shuffled over to join his buddy, rubbing his throat as he went.

"So who are you guys?" Havranek repeated. "We deserve some answers."

"So do we," said Frank. "About steroids, and Bobby Walker's death, and point-shaving, for a start."

Elvin Jackson took a step forward, his fists clenched, his face distorted with anger. Frank braced himself for another attack.

"Don't ever accuse us of throwing games!" Jackson shouted. "It's a dirty lie!"

"We're not accusing either of you," Joe told him. "But you must have seen what's going on. You guys are co-captains of the team. You have to know!"

Havranek stared at the ground and muttered, "That's team business, for us to deal with in our own way."

"You *haven't* dealt with it, and the Sharks are about to go down the drain," Frank pointed out. He decided to take a risk. "That's why Nicky Chambers asked us for help."

"Nicky?" Jackson said, looking surprised. "What does he have to do with it?"

"Look, you'd better meet our dad," Frank replied. "He can explain what's going on better than we can."

The two Sharks checked with each other, as if wondering whether this was some new trick.

"Listen, Rich," Joe said, extending his open hands. "I'll go in your car, and one of you can ride with Frank. We're your friends—really."

Jackson looked at Joe, then met Frank's eyes and nodded. "Okay," he said. "We'll take a chance."

Fenton Hardy was on the phone when Joe and Frank walked into the living room with their two visitors. He hung up and stood to greet them.

"Dad, I want you to meet two guys who can

help us," Joe said. "This is Elvin Jackson and Rich 'Racehorse' Havranek."

Fenton shook hands with the two athletes. "It's a pleasure," he said. "You men have given me a lot over the years."

"Dad," Frank said, "we think it's time to let them in on what we're doing."

Fenton looked into his elder son's eyes and then into the faces of Jackson and Havranek. He was silent for a moment as he pondered this new twist in a complicated case.

"Fine," he said. "Why don't you gentlemen have a seat. Joe, would you make some coffee?"

Over the next few minutes Fenton outlined the scope of the investigation without going into details. He told the players about Nicky Chambers's concerns and Peter Hyde's shady business dealings.

"What I suspect," Fenton concluded, "is that Peter Hyde's Las Vegas connections go a long way toward explaining what's happened to your team."

Joe brought in the coffeepot with cups and saucers. He poured for the five of them.

Rich Havranek took a sip of coffee. "I think you're right on track, Mr. Hardy," he said, "but there's a lot you don't know."

"And that's why you're here," Frank said. "You can help us fill in some of the blanks."

Elvin Jackson stood up and walked slowly to the glass door leading to the balcony. He stared out into the night, his big quarterback's hands in the pockets of his slacks. "It all started when Bobby died," he said in a low voice, his back still to the room.

"He knew about steroids, how dangerous they are," Jackson continued. "But there was big money involved. Melissa Sharpe wanted Doc Washington to produce supermen who would sell lots of her shoes. And steroids make supermen, for a while at least."

"Were you two on steroids—along with Bobby?" Fenton asked softly.

"Yeah," Jackson said, turning his grim face toward Fenton. "For a while. And Bobby—well, he and Jennifer were tight. They even planned to be married. He was probably the first of the Sharks that Melissa lined up through Jennifer. But Bobby was hurting. The pills were messing with his head, making him crazy. I saw him that afternoon, the day he died, when he drove into the parking lot. He was yelling at Jennifer about how he was going to report what was happening to the league authorities. And then he took off in his car."

Rich Havranek picked up the story. "Jennifer came running to El and me. She said he was strung out on pills and that he was headed for L.A., so we took off after him up the Coast Highway. We caught up with him at about the same . . ." Havranek's voice broke, and he brushed his hand across his eyes before going on. "At about the same spot we caught up with you guys tonight. Before we could stop him, his car went off the road, rolled, and blew up. Bobby never had a chance."

Havranek looked down at his hands. Jackson was staring into the dark again. No one spoke.

"We ran," Jackson said softly. "We fled the scene of the accident."

"But it wasn't your fault," Joe said. "Why didn't you tell the authorities what happened?"

"At first we were afraid we'd have to open up about taking steroids," Havranek explained. "But the next day we went to Jennifer Washington and told her everything. Turns out, she taped us talking about Bobby and the crash and the pills—you see, she's in it with Hyde and Melissa. If they made the tape public, we could have kissed our careers goodbye."

"Look," Jackson said, sighing deeply. "All we ever wanted was to play football, but now we're in so deep it's hard to see how to get out. The Syndicate is holding that tape over our heads. They know we don't dare go to league authorities with what we know about guys throwing games."

"And we aren't the only ones," Havranek added. "Lot of cats are in the same trap."

"Are you still on steroids?" Frank asked.

"No way," Havranek said. "El's not either."

"Man, I've seen guys do some weird things on 'roids," Jackson said. "Go into 'roid rages, beat up their buddies"—he glanced at Joe—"throw tables through restaurant windows. You couldn't force one of those pills down my throat. No way."

"But see, to the Syndicate that doesn't matter," Havranek added. "Our careers are in their hands. They can ruin us anytime they want to."

"What about point-shaving?" Fenton asked.

"It's happening," Jackson said, tight-jawed. "But it's hard to prove. Everybody makes a mistake now and then, sometimes at the worst possible time. Who can say for sure whether it's an accident or not?"

"So do we go to the D.A.?" Joe asked. "Can he make a case against Hyde and the others?"

"Not yet," Fenton Hardy. "We're still looking for solid evidence that can be presented to a jury."

He looked at Jackson and at Havranek. "I want to thank you men," he said. "What you did tonight wasn't easy."

"There's one more thing I think you'd better know, Mr. Hardy," Rich said as he and Jackson stood up to go. "Joe is a tough kid, and a pretty good ball player. But football's a dangerous sport, especially if somebody's out to get you."

"Rich is right," Jackson added. "What happened to Joe today was just a warning. People like Hyde will stop at nothing."

Chapter 12

IT WAS GETTING LATE, and Joe had a game to play the next day. At least he hoped he did. He knew how deeply his teammates' warnings had affected his father. Would Fenton make Joe stay out of the game? Joe closed the door behind Havranek and Jackson and waited with a sinking heart to hear the verdict.

Fenton Hardy was standing at the door to the balcony, staring out into the night. Frank sat at the table looking at the stack of papers his father had compiled in Washington and in Las Vegas.

Fenton turned around and looked at Joe. "I've filled in another piece of the puzzle," he said. "You both need to hear this before we decide what to do next. I managed to find someone who was part of the crew on Hyde's yacht the night Ruskin disappeared."

"How did you find him?" Joe asked. He pulled out a chair and sat at the table across from Frank. Fenton continued to stand.

"He's been working on a tuna boat sailing out of San Diego for the last several years," Fenton explained. "I had the crew manifest for Hyde's yacht, so I was able to track him down through the seamen's union. It didn't take too much persuasion to get him to talk. He said his conscience has been bothering him ever since that night on the high seas. That's who I was talking to on the phone when you walked in tonight."

"What did he tell you?" Frank asked.

"He said he wasn't able to sleep that night, so he went up on deck for a smoke. He saw Walter Ruskin leaning against the rail, just staring out at the ocean. Then came the incredible part. A man in scuba gear surfaced next to the yacht, sneaked up a ladder, grabbed Ruskin by the ankles, and pulled him into the water. Ruskin didn't even have time to call for help. A few minutes later my sailor friend saw the frogman climb aboard the ship."

"Did he see who it was?" Joe asked eagerly.

Fenton nodded. "Yes, he did. When the assassin took off his mask, the sailor saw that he was Hyde's bodyguard. A few days later, when the yacht docked at Mauritius, in the Indian

Ocean, the bodyguard went ashore and never returned."

"What a story!" Frank exclaimed. "Do you think your sailor friend will be willing to testify?"

"He told me he would," Fenton replied. "But to what? He can't swear that Peter Hyde had anything to do with it. And in any case, he's deathly afraid of Peter Hyde. After hearing his story, I suspect he has good reason to be."

"So it all comes down to the game tomorrow," Frank said. He looked across the table at his brother. "Joe's got to play, Dad. And we've got to stay on Hyde's trail."

"It's your call, son," Fenton said. "You heard what your two teammates said. If I had my choice—well, I don't know. In any case, I'm leaving it up to you."

The phone rang. Frank walked over to the kitchen counter and picked up the receiver. "Oh, hi, Rich," he said. "No, we're still up." He listened for a while and then laughed. "Good for you! And good luck tomorrow."

"What did he say?" Joe asked eagerly.

"He and Elvin were hoping that Dad will hold off going to the police with his evidence until after the game tomorrow. He said if you couldn't do that, they'd understand. But, Dad, he said to tell you that if you can wait, the people of San

Diego will see a whale of a game tomorrow afternoon, a game they'll never forget."

Frank grinned. "He also said, 'If I see House McMaran make one mistake tomorrow, I'll kick his big ol' ugly rear end from here to San Francisco. We're going out winners.' "

"All right!" Joe shouted. "And so am I!"

Fenton shook his head and rolled his eyes. "What did I expect?" he murmured.

Late as it was, Joe realized that he was too excited to sleep. "Let's take a walk on the beach," he suggested to Frank. "I need to wind down."

"I'm going to bed," Fenton said. "Be sure to lock up when you come in."

The brothers pulled on sweaters, took the elevator downstairs, and walked across the street to the beach. The stars shone brightly, and they could see the skyline of downtown San Diego in the distance. Out in the bay a couple of yachts, their lights twinkling, rode the gentle swells. The only sound was the gentle, rhythmic rumble of the surf.

"Are you nervous?" Frank asked as they started across the sand.

"Who, me? Nervous?" Joe said. "What a ridiculous idea. No, I'm not nervous. I'm scared to death!"

As they strolled along the wet sand, just above the reach of the incoming waves, Joe picked up a flat stone and skipped it across the surface.

"It's not that I'm scared of getting hurt," he continued thoughtfully. "I mean, what happened today was pretty bad, but I took it and I survived. What I'm really scared of is messing up. I don't want to look like a fumble-fingered idiot."

"Is the coach still having you call for the fair catch every time?" Frank asked.

"He sure is," Joe replied, not hiding the disgust he felt. "It's enough to make me boil. But what about you, Frank? You sound—I don't know. Worried, I guess."

"I am," Frank said. "I'm worried that the Syndicate knows we're closing in on them and is planning to do something desperate. From what Dad told us, Hyde and his gang have put everything on tomorrow's game. They'll stop at nothing to make sure the Sharks lose. I hope security is tight at the stadium."

"Mr. Chambers told Dad it would be," Joe said. "What about Rosen? Do you think he'll testify against Hyde?"

"Rosen's somebody who'll do whatever it takes to save his own hide," Frank answered. "Oops, sorry—bad joke. Anyway, we've got the goods on him. But he's just a cog in the wheel, and a small cog at that. He said so himself. Hyde spots a person's weakness and uses it for his own ends. Rosen's weakness is gambling. He's in Hyde's debt, so he does as Hyde tells him. He's more weak than wicked, if you ask me."

"This case just keeps getting more complex, doesn't it?" Joe mused. "A guy skimming money off a team's endorsement contracts, a trainer pushing steroids, a bunch of pro football players shaving points and even throwing games—not to mention a high-powered businesswoman who's in on the deal somehow. You think we're ready to run with it?"

Frank chuckled. "You're the kick return expert, Joe. Before you run with it, you have to catch the ball. And even then you need good blocking and a certain amount of luck if you expect to score. But yes, I'm feeling good about this case. Another day, maybe two, and we'll wrap it up."

"I hope so," Joe said. "You know what I don't understand? How can some bozo like House McMaran mess up a beautiful game like football? When I'm out there playing, I'm in another world. It doesn't matter whether it's in Pacific Rim Stadium or our backyard. It's a thrill. And here's House McMaran getting paid a ton of money to have that kind of fun, but he's willing to ruin it for everybody. Forget the big bucks. Millions of guys would *pay* to do what he's doing."

"Like Havranek and Jackson," Frank said. "They're not playing for money, they're playing for the love of the game. If they had to, they'd play for nothing."

Joe looked out toward the western horizon, then paused and frowned. "Look, Frank," he said. "Some guy's just now coming in from a scuba dive. I didn't know people went out after dark."

"I didn't either," Frank said. "Funny."

The diver was just fifteen or twenty yards from shore, lifting his flippers high as he waddled through the surf. By the glow from the streetlights behind him, Joe could see that he was wearing a diving mask and wet suit and carrying a spear gun.

"He's pretty big, isn't he?" Frank said. "Maybe the Sharks ought to sign him to replace McMaran."

Joe was about to respond with a joke when he saw the diver raise his spear gun, aim it at his chest, and pull the trigger.

"Wha—" Joe felt a stinging sensation on his right side, just over his ribs. It was no more painful than a bee sting. Shocked, he looked down and saw a small yellow-tailed dart protruding from his shirt. He started to reach for it, to pull it out, but at that moment an electric charge surged through his body. He fell to the ground, totally immobilized.

As he lay there, unable to move, he saw the huge diver swing at Frank, hitting him squarely on the chin. Frank fell. His attacker hoisted Frank onto his shoulder like a sack of potatoes. Then he turned and carried Frank back into the surf.

Chapter 13

FRANK WANTED to open his eyes, but when he did, the walls seemed to be moving. He felt dizzy and very tired. He opened his mouth to yawn and suddenly noticed that his chin ached. Touching it carefully, just to the left of his lower lip, he could feel a tender spot caked with dried blood. He didn't think anything was broken. He closed his eyes and drifted off again.

The next time he woke up, someone was touching his chin with a warm, damp cloth. He opened his eyes and saw a tall, dark woman sitting beside him on the narrow bunk. From Joe's description, he guessed that this was Jennifer Washington. She looked worried.

"You're Frank, aren't you?" she asked.

"Joe's brother. Melissa Sharpe told me. I'm glad you're finally waking up."

"Where am I?" Frank asked. He was lying on a bunk of some sort in a small room with rich mahogany-colored walls. There was an open porthole, but through it he could see only darkness. A ship, he thought, seizing the idea as if it were a life preserver. He was on a ship.

"This is the *Dr. Jekyll,*" Washington said. "Peter Hyde's yacht."

"Where are we going?" Frank asked. "And what does Hyde want with me?"

"We're not going anywhere for now, but we've charted a course for the Indian Ocean," Washington said. "For the island of Mauritius. If all goes as planned, we'll have ourselves a nice little vacation for a few days. If not? Well, then we'll have ourselves a nice little life on a lovely tropical isle. Either way, we'll be sailing right after the game."

"What do you want with me?" Frank asked. "And what did you do to my brother?"

"No more questions," she said briskly. "It'll be light soon, and Mr. Hyde would like to see you in his stateroom before he leaves. You can freshen up in there." She pointed toward a door near the bed.

"Wait," Frank said. "There's something I don't understand."

"What is it?" she asked impatiently.

"I don't understand how you could be doing

this," Frank said. "I mean the steroids and everything."

"There's no scientific proof that anabolic steroids are harmful to the human body—at least not when they're taken in strictly controlled amounts," Washington said. She sounded like an automaton.

"I wonder if Bobby Walker would agree?" Frank asked in a soft voice.

"You leave Bobby out of this," Washington said, her eyes blazing. "And you'd better watch your mouth, because you don't know what Peter Hyde is capable of doing. Now get in there and clean yourself up."

Frank stepped into the compact little bathroom and washed his face, careful not to touch his chin. Examining his face in the mirror, he decided that the gash probably wouldn't need stitches. He returned to the cabin, and then followed Washington down the narrow companionway to a room that took up the whole width of the yacht, where she left him. The floor was covered with thick yellow carpet, interwoven with intricate oriental designs. A fireplace was set into one wall, and on either side there were built-in bookshelves filled with old leather-bound volumes. Chairs and a sofa covered in light brown velvet were arranged near the fireplace. Modern abstract paintings adorned the walls.

A tall, balding man dressed in white flannel

slacks and a blue silk blazer looked up. "Ah—Frank Hardy, I believe," he said, in what Frank decided was a terribly phony English accent.

Frank waited silently.

"I've just learned that you are one of my employees," Hyde continued. "Such a small world, is it not?"

"You won't get away with this," Frank said.

"Oh, bravo, Mr. Hardy," Hyde said with a big smile. "Ever since my childhood Saturday afternoons at the cinema, I have dreamed of hearing someone deliver that line in real life. And you said it with such conviction, too."

He picked up a carved ivory box from a table and examined it, then continued. "In any case, I'm afraid I *shall* get away with it and in no more than a day or two. It isn't often that a man achieves his lifelong dream. Mine has been to dominate the sports entertainment industry, and now I am only a step away from making that dream a reality."

"You'll get caught," Frank snapped.

"Impossible," Hyde replied smoothly. "As you should know by now, young man, I leave nothing to chance—not nervous-Nelly underlings like Andrew Rosen, or even my bets. Already half the members of the Sharks team do as I tell them. So does their trainer. And as soon as they lose this afternoon, Nicky Chambers will be forced to sell the team. Of course, when he signs the Sharks over to the Syndicate, he won't know he's actually dealing with me. Nonetheless, *I'll* own the whole team. The Sharks will play by my rules, not the league's, and they'll be the most successful franchise in America. It won't be long until I become one of the richest men in the world."

"What do you want with me?" Frank asked.

"You're Joe Hardy's brother, aren't you?" Hyde said, an ugly smile twisting his lips. "That's right, Frank. Nothing slips by me. I've had several men tracking you down—and the trail led to a town called Bayport." He laughed. "Quite an interesting family you have—and involved in such a fascinating line of work."

"So what are you going to do with me?" Frank pressed.

"You're insurance," Hyde told him. "Your father knows you're here. As long as they do nothing foolish, such as going to the police, you'll be fine. Mr. Chambers and the Syndicate will get the little transaction taken care of, and you'll be back safe and sound in your dear little Bayport."

"What about Joe?" Frank asked. "What did you do to him?"

"He's perfectly fine," Hyde answered, "although he may still be feeling a little tingle. And as long as he stays out of the flow of play tomorrow, he'll be fine. He simply has to remember that we have his older brother. What choice does he have but to play along?"

Frank felt a stab of fear. Hyde was being too open with him. He would never admit so much unless he knew that he could count on Frank's silence—his *permanent* silence.

Jennifer Washington came into the room. With her was Melissa Sharpe.

"Allow me to introduce the other half of the Syndicate," Hyde said with a theatrical sweep of his arm.

Sharpe, wearing white slacks and a white sweater, lowered herself into one of the velvet chairs and nodded gracefully. "Hello, Frank," she said.

Frank gave her a scathing look.

"I know this is difficult," she began slowly, "but I want you to know that I appreciate your kindness toward Sandy," she said. "She's told me how much she likes you."

"Does she know about all this?" Frank asked.

"She knows nothing, I assure you," Sharpe said. "If all goes as planned, she never will."

"I don't understand," Frank said. "Don't you love your daughter? How can you be involved with someone like Peter Hyde? What will she think of you when she finds out you're the partner of a crook?"

"I'm involved with Pete Hyde *because* of my daughter," Melissa Sharpe answered impatiently. "Peter rescued me a long, long time ago. I was so far down, I had decided life wasn't worth living." She glanced at Hyde, her eyes shining with gratitude. "Peter gave me a reason to live. Everything I have, everything I've been able to give Sandy, I owe to him. And now this wonderful, brilliant man is going to make sure that I'll never want for anything in my life. And neither will Sandy."

Frank just stared at Melissa Sharpe. He was imagining how hurt Sandy would be. She didn't deserve the pain she was about to experience. He shook his head sadly.

"I didn't really expect you to understand," Sharpe said.

Just then Jennifer Washington went over to the wet bar at the side of the cabin. When she turned and approached Frank, she had a glass filled with a clear liquid in her hand. "Drink this," she told him.

"Thanks, but I'm not thirsty," Frank replied.

"I didn't ask if you were thirsty. I told you to drink this," Washington repeated. From the pocket of her jacket, she pulled a snub-nosed revolver.

Frank drank it. There was a bitter aftertaste.

"That's better," Hyde commented blandly. He was standing in front of the fireplace now, inspecting what appeared to be a high-tech camera with a telephoto lens.

"Mr. Hardy," Hyde said jovially. "Come over here and let me show you something." He held up the camera.

But as Frank looked more closely, he saw that it wasn't a camera at all. He saw that Hyde had his finger around a trigger at the base of what he had assumed was the lens. He was looking at a gun, a silencer-equipped automatic weapon disguised as a camera.

"It's a beauty, isn't it?" Hyde said, smiling. "One of the fortunate by-products of the cold war. It shoots lethal poison darts. The Bulgarian secret police were particularly adept at using this innovative little item. The trigger releases the dart, it barely penetrates the skin, and then the dart drops out. The victim dies within seconds of an apparent heart attack. It leaves no mark on the skin, no traces in the body. Neither the victim nor the coroner ever knows the real cause of death."

"I suppose you want me to ask who it's for?" Frank said grimly. He was beginning to feel dizzy. He was having trouble focusing on Hyde, so he backed into the couch and sat down heavily.

"No matter whether you ask," Hyde said, smiling and seeming to ignore Frank's condition. "Let's just call it our Shark Shooter.

Athletes in the heat of competition have been known to have heart attacks, even young athletes like your brother. It's a shame, but it happens. We'll have it aimed at young Number Thirteen every minute he's on the field."

Chapter

14

JOE WALKED into the crowded Sharks dressing room on Sunday morning and noticed his Number Thirteen jersey hanging in his locker. He found himself wondering if he should have switched numbers.

Not that he had ever been superstitious. Sure, he sometimes wore the same pair of baseball socks in game after game, without washing them, when Bayport was on a winning streak. And he always had hot tea, a bowl of pasta, and a banana before football games. That didn't mean he was superstitious.

But now, after what had happened the night before, Joe was wishing for a rabbit's foot or some other lucky charm. He needed any good luck he could find. Where was Frank? What had happened to him? In his mind's eye Joe kept seeing a monster in scuba gear, knocking out his brother and carrying him into the sea.

The weapon had stunned Joe for at least ten minutes. Still conscious, he had lain flat on his back, unable to move, until the tide started to come in, and cold water washed in tiny rivulets around his body. Finally he managed to stagger to his feet and make his way back to the apartment.

The call had come several hours later. Fenton had picked up the receiver, holding it so that Joe, too, could hear.

"Your son is safe," a woman's voice had said. "For now. But do not go to the police. Do nothing, and everything will be all right." Then came a click, followed by a dial tone.

At the moment the locker room was crowded with visitors, reporters, and team officials. The Sharks themselves were unusually quiet as they got ready to play what they all knew would be the biggest game of the year, perhaps the biggest game in the history of the franchise.

Joe felt as if he were in a trance. He pulled on a gray T-shirt and skintight silver game pants with the teal-colored stripe running down each leg. Then he walked over to a training table, hoisted himself up, and sat with his legs stretched out while a trainer taped his ankles.

Once his ankles were securely wrapped, Joe

went back to the bench in front of his locker and pulled on the long, teal-colored stockings the Sharks wore. A new pair of white socks went on top of them.

Rich Havranek sat down beside him and slapped him on the thigh pad. "Nervous, kid?" the big running back asked.

Joe nodded. He was afraid his voice would fail him if he tried to say a word.

"Me, too," Havranek said. "But a while back I finally figured out that being nervous helps you stay mentally sharp, so I don't worry about it anymore. And once you get out there and hit somebody—or get hit—it all goes away."

Nicky Chambers walked into the dressing room. He moved among his players, talking quietly to them, wishing them luck. Joe saw him coming his way. He had to decide what to do.

Chambers shook his hand. "Good luck, son," he said. "I've got all the confidence in the world in you."

"Mr. Chambers, can we speak privately for a minute?"

"Sure, son," the Sharks owner said. They walked down the hall together to Coach Landers's office. It was empty. They stepped inside and closed the door.

"Mr. Chambers, Frank's been kidnapped,"

Joe said. He watched the older man's face go white as soon as he uttered the words.

Joe went on to explain quickly what had happened. He repeated the warning that the police shouldn't be informed. "But I felt that I had to tell you," Joe said, "just in case something happened during the game."

"I'm glad you did," Chambers said. "If it makes you feel any better, you should know that I took certain precautions. Our security is the tightest it's ever been."

Chambers stayed in the coach's office to make a phone call to his chief of security. Joe walked back down the hall to the dressing room. He could hear the distant rumble of the crowd filing into the stadium, but he was also aware of another sound, a loud clanging noise coming from somewhere near the showers. It sounded as if someone were trying to open his locker with a fire ax.

Joe walked quietly in that direction. Just around a corner he saw House McMaran, in game pants and no shirt, banging his head with fearsome force into a badly dented locker. Over and over he drove his head against the metal door. He acted completely crazed.

Joe backed away, but not before McMaran noticed him. The huge lineman's eyes were so ferocious that Joe felt a cold chill run down his back. He realized that this wild-eyed, red-faced creature staring at him was capable of anything. Even murder.

Several minutes later a guard cleared the visitors out of the dressing room, and Coach Landers stood before a chalk board. He wore a black baseball cap with a Sharks insignia on the front, a handsome black sweater, and gray slacks. On his feet were black turf shoes. "Okay, men, listen up," he said. "Pregame warm-up in five minutes, back in here at twelve-thirty, kickoff at one o'clock sharp."

Joe laced up his shoulder pads, pulled his black jersey over his head, and turned his back to Elvin Jackson. The quarterback helped him pull his jersey down over his pads. Joe did the same for Jackson. Taking their silver helmets out of their cubicles, the Sharks clattered up the runway toward the bright sunshine, with the team captains, Jackson and Havranek, leading the way.

A roar erupted as the team trotted onto the field. It was still nearly an hour before game time, but Joe saw that the stadium was nearly full. Sharks fans knew how vital this game was. They had probably read the same headline in the morning paper that Joe had seen: "Chambers to Sell Sharks if Toros Win."

Joe scanned the crowd. Among those many thousands, was there an assassin watching him? There were police stationed at all the entrances and high atop the stadium on the press box roof. Chambers hadn't been kidding when he said that security was tight. The question was, was it tight enough?

As the Sharks went through their limbering-up exercises, Joe sneaked a glance toward the other end of the field. The Toros looked big. They wore what one of their captains had called their "good luck threads," yellow pants and white jerseys. Their gold helmets were emblazoned in blue with the horns of a bull. They were coming into San Diego with the confidence born of a six-game winning streak.

Joe lined up with his fellow kick returners to field Bobby Joe Ratliff's warm-up punts. "Watch the wind," Coach Westcott reminded them. "Midafternoon, it'll start swirling. You jokers are going to have to concentrate."

The warm-up ended, and the players returned to the dressing room. Coach Landers called them together before the chalkboard for a last-minute review of strategy.

"Men, I don't have to remind you how important this game is," he said forcefully at the end of his talk. "If we lose today, we can kiss the playoffs goodbye. You all know that we're a better team than those bums. So get out there and show them what the San Diego Sharks are made of."

"Coach?" Elvin Jackson said, as the team started to move out. "Could you give us a moment?"

Landers stepped out of the room. Jackson, helmet in hand, stood quietly looking into the eyes of men who had followed him into many battles over the years. They looked back at him with deep respect, waiting for what he had to say.

"We've had a hard season," Jackson said quietly, his deep voice commanding attention. "You know it as well as I do. We've been fighting among ourselves instead of fighting our opponents. That's over. Beginning this very minute, we're in this together. I want to walk off that field this evening knowing that everybody in this room gave his best. For the next three hours, that's all that matters. We'll solve our problems later. Right now, we've got a game to play."

With a deep, guttural roar, the team voiced its agreement.

"One more thing," the quarterback said. "A lot of you here played with Bobby Walker. The man's been on my mind lately. I want you to think about Bobby when you're out there today. I want you to play as if he's watching us today. Try to make him proud."

The Sharks started shouting and pounding each other on the back. As they surged out the door and up the runway, their cleats clattering on the concrete, Joe wondered who among them were traitors. He looked into their faces as they waited to take the field, but he couldn't tell.

The encouragement from Landers and Jackson apparently worked. The Sharks kicked off to Los Angeles, and the Toros' return man barely made it out to his own five-yard line. The next three plays netted a total of three yards. The Toros had to punt.

"Remember, Hardy, fair catch, no matter what," Landers reminded Joe as the jubilant Sharks defensive unit came racing off the field. Jogging onto the field, Joe buckled his chin strap, put in his mouthpiece, and waited for the punt at midfield. His mouth was dry, his stomach hollow. He could see the Toros punter standing at the back of his own end zone waiting for the snap of the ball. Twice the punter looked back to make sure his feet were inside the line. The stadium was a cauldron of sound. The Sharks fans were on their feet, shouting and stamping in rhythm.

Waiting on the fifty-yard line, Joe couldn't hear the punter calling signals, but he saw the punter swing his leg into the ball just before the Sharks linemen forced their way through the block. Joe searched the sky for the ball and realized that one of his teammates must have grazed it with a fingertip. The ball, wavering in the air, was going to fall much shorter than Joe had anticipated.

Joe dashed forward, his eye on the fluttering

football. Since the Sharks had gone for the block, the Toros' contain men were racing up the field untouched. They were on him, in his face, trying to unnerve him and make him miss.

"Your mama catches better than you do!" one of them shouted as Joe raised his arm for the fair catch.

Once the Toros saw the fair catch signal, they couldn't touch Joe. But they did their best to make him miss the catch. They clustered around him, yelling in his ears and waiting for him to fumble.

Joe didn't fumble. He watched the ball sail into his chest, fell to his knees, and laughed.

That was the start of a magnificent offensive drive. Joe watched from the sidelines as Elvin Jackson, from the thirty, faked to his left and swung a quick pass to Havranek coming out of the backfield. The big, fast running back broke three tackles, tightroped his way down the sideline, and carried two Toros into the end zone. The crowd went crazy. So did Havranek's fellow Sharks.

Jackson was magnificent, not only with his passing, but with his play-calling. Walking up to the line, he seemed to have X-ray vision. Joe watched, amazed, as time after time the veteran quarterback spotted a weakness in the Toros' defense and checked off at the line. His new play worked almost every time.

The Toros, seeing a spot in the playoffs almost in their grasp, refused to roll over and play dead. With two minutes to go in the half, the score was tied at 17. The crowd was on its feet in a frenzy.

The Toros had the ball on their own thirty. Facing a third down and six to go for a first down, the Toros' quarterback gazed upfield, realized he had to scramble, and soon found himself wrapped in the massive arms of three Sharks defensive linemen. He was sacked for a ten-yard loss. The Toros would have to punt. As Joe trotted onto the field, the Sharks' defensive unit exited to a standing ovation.

Joe waited for the punt at his own thirty. Again, the noise of the crowd was so loud that he couldn't hear the punter calling signals. He couldn't hear the *thwack* of the ball as the punter swung the top of his foot into it. He watched the football floating high, silhouetted against a brilliant sky. At the top of its arc, he saw it flutter in the wind, and he could sense several Toros coming close. As he raised his arms, he realized with horror that he had misjudged the ball's flight. It grazed his fingertips and bounced away crazily. Desperately, he dived into a nest of Toros, all scrambling for the elusive football.

As he saw a white-shirted Toro pull the ball into his chest, Joe pounded his fist against the ground in an agony of frustration. Then he looked up to see House McMaran looming above the pileup of players, with a nasty grin on his face.

"Way to go, butterfingers," House said, in a voice too low to be overheard. "Now you're playing our game."

Chapter 15

JOE'S MISTAKE gave the Toros a chance to kick a field goal with ten seconds left on the clock. The Sharks left the field at halftime trailing by three, 20–17. As they walked into the dressing room, Joe could hear a thunder of boos. No one had to tell him they were aimed at him.

To his great relief, Coach Landers didn't seem overly concerned. "Look, Joe made a mistake, a rookie mistake," he told the Sharks when they had assembled in front of the chalkboard. "Nobody feels worse about it than he does."

"Hey, little buddy, these things happen, don't they?" House McMaran commented. He was standing against the wall behind Coach Landers. He winked at Joe.

Joe glanced at Jackson and then at Havranek. Neither would return his glance. He wondered if they still had lingering suspicions about his loyalty, despite the long talk the night before.

He thought of Frank. Was that why he had dropped the ball? Had he been worrying about his brother instead of concentrating on the game? How long could he stand the agony of not knowing what had happened to Frank? To distract himself, he tried to focus on what the coach was saying.

Finally halftime ended, and the team started up the runway toward the field. Joe put himself in the middle of the pack. That way, maybe the fans wouldn't notice him.

Crazy Legs Westcott fell into step next to him. "Know what you do when you fall off a horse?" he asked.

"Get back on again?" Joe replied.

"That's what I hear," Westcott said. "Not that you're going to get me on a horse to find out. Anyway, kid, just shake it off. You'll be all right."

Aboard the *Dr. Jekyll,* Frank was desperately trying to wake up. He felt as if he were underwater, fighting through tangled strands of kelp to push his way to the light. Opening his eyes, he found himself tangled in the sheets of his narrow bunk. He knew without a doubt what had happened. Jennifer Washington had drugged him. He pushed himself to his feet and stumbled across the cabin to the door. It was locked. Then he moved to the porthole. From the angle of the sun, he knew it must be after noon. What was happening to Joe? Frank felt a wave of claustrophobic panic sweep over him. He wanted to beat his fists against the wall. But that wouldn't help Joe. What he had to do was figure out a way to escape.

Suddenly he heard a buzzing sound that got louder and louder, until it was a full roar. Frank identified it as a helicopter landing on the deck of the yacht. Most likely it had come to pick up Hyde and Sharpe, to take them to the stadium and the luxurious sky box owned by Hyde-Ruskin.

A few moments passed and the helicopter took off again. From his porthole, Frank saw it turn toward the mainland, looking like a giant grasshopper. He imagined that he saw Melissa Sharpe's face at one of the windows. Never had he felt so helpless.

He knew he wasn't alone on the yacht. He had seen a couple of crew members when he'd gone into Hyde's stateroom. One of them had been carrying an assault rifle and looked as if he knew how to use it. It wouldn't help Joe if Frank tried something and was shot. But he couldn't simply sit and wait.

What about Jennifer Washington? Had she

left in the chopper, too? Just as Frank wondered this, he heard a key in the lock. The door swung open and Washington ducked in, then shut it carefully.

"You've got to get off this boat," she said in a panicky voice.

Frank couldn't believe what she said next. "Hyde is planning to kill your brother and fix it so it looks like a heart attack. He promised me no one would be hurt, but he was lying. And I won't be a party to cold-blooded murder. There's been too much death already."

Frank knew she was referring to Bobby Walker, and felt a chill run down his spine. "Look, you've got to help me," he said. "Just let me out of this cabin, and I'll figure out what to do next."

"I can't," Washington said, struggling to control her voice. "Hyde's guard is patrolling the deck. He'd shoot us both."

"Where's the gun you had last night?" Frank asked.

"Right here," Washington said, taking the revolver out of the pocket of her warm-up jacket. "But it's not loaded. It wasn't loaded then, either. And I don't have any bullets for it."

"Is there a life raft on board? Can I swim to shore?" Frank asked desperately.

"Of course, there's a life raft," Washington said, "but what's the use? You'd be a sitting duck. And it's too far to swim, even if the guard didn't see you."

"Then what?" Frank asked. He sat down hard on the edge of the bunk, his head in his hands.

"The boat!" Washington said, slapping her hand against the door. "Why didn't I think of it sooner? Hyde's cigarette boat, the one he uses for waterskiing, is tied up at the stern. The key is usually on a hook in the engine room. You stay here. I'll be right back."

She locked him in again, and Frank started pacing. Was this a trick? How far could he trust her?

Minutes later she was back with an ignition key.

"Great! Let's go," Frank exclaimed.

"Not yet," Washington replied. "We have to wait until the guard is up at the bow. That way, we may have time."

The wait seemed endless. To distract himself, Frank asked, "How did you get mixed up with Hyde in the first place?"

Washington sighed. "It's a long story," she replied. "Ever since Bobby's death, I've been as much a prisoner as you are. A prisoner of Peter Hyde. Basically I've been pushing pills for the Syndicate, even though it goes against everything I believe. But I felt I had to. Hearing Hyde's plans for your brother was the last straw, though. We may not get off this boat alive, but at this point I really don't care."

She was quiet for a moment, and Frank could see that she was trying to hold back her tears.

There were footsteps overhead. Washington held up a hand for silence. As the footsteps faded, she pointed to the door.

"Now!" she whispered. "Follow me."

They raced down a narrow passageway and out onto the stern of the yacht. As they came out the doorway, Frank ran headlong into another guard.

The guard and Frank fell in a tangle onto the deck. The guard's assault rifle slipped from his hands and slid out of his reach. Frank was the first to scramble to his feet. As the guard reached for his weapon, Frank gave it a kick that sent it skittering across the deck and over the side.

"Get to the boat!" Frank shouted as Washington raced past him. The guard grabbed for her, but Frank landed a karate kick to his jaw that sent the man staggering against the railing. Frank followed him, grabbed the man's foot with both hands, and flipped him over the waist-high rail. He hit the water with a splash and went under.

Frank raced to the stern and leapt into the boat. "You take the wheel!" Washington shouted, trying to keep her balance in the rocking boat. She handed Frank the key and untied the line. Frank turned the ignition, and the engine sputtered, then roared to life. They began backing away from the yacht.

"Stay down!" Frank shouted as he shoved the lever into low gear. He could see the guard in the water pulling himself back aboard the yacht. As they cleared the gleaming white ship, he glanced over his shoulder. The other guard was running along the deck toward the stern, raising his rifle to fire. Washington was shrugging on a bright orange life jacket. She tossed one to Frank, too.

It seemed as if they were only a mile or so outside La Jolla Cove. Had it been only a week earlier that he and Joe had enjoyed a carefree game of touch football on the green grass above the cove?

The sleek, powerful cigarette boat was fast, but Frank knew it couldn't outrun a bullet. His only hope was that the guard would not be able to hit his target. Looking back, he saw the guard taking aim. Frank tried to stay as low in the boat as possible as it bounced over the waves.

A bullet whizzed past Jennifer's shoulder and shattered the boat's windshield. Frank heard the ringing sound of metal being punctured. Turning, he saw a neat hole in the motor, just before a sound as loud as thunder engulfed him. A blast of searing wind threw him over the prow of the boat. In a great orange ball of fire, the cigarette boat exploded.

Chapter 16

"JENNIFER!" FRANK SHOUTED, then coughed as he swallowed a mouthful of salt water. Treading water, he watched what was left of the speedboat burn. The flames hissed when they touched the water. There was no sign of Washington.

Frank kicked off his shoes and swam closer to the slowly burning hulk. A gust of wind briefly cleared away the smoke. Washington was on the other side of the boat, feebly moving her arms. Her eyes were closed.

Frank swam over to her and held her head out of the water. Over her shoulder, in the distance, he could see the yacht beginning to turn to sail toward them. The shore was no more than a hundred yards away, and the explosion of the cigarette boat would surely bring the Coast Guard to the scene. "Can you swim?" Frank asked.

Washington nodded. "I think so," she gasped.

A few minutes later they staggered through the rolling surf onto a narrow beach. Frank spotted a small parking lot and a paved road leading up the hill and realized where they were. The road led up to the university campus. Wet, cold, and exhausted, he and Washington struggled up the hill to busy Torrey Pines Road and found a phone booth. Frank dug into the pocket of his wet jeans and found a quarter. As he dialed Sandy's number, he muttered to himself, "Please, please be there!"

Sandy answered the phone. "Frank, where in the world are you?" she demanded. "Are you okay?"

"Not exactly," Frank replied. "Can you come pick me up, right away?"

In ten minutes Sandy was there and shocked by Frank's bedraggled appearance. She was clearly surprised to see Jennifer Washington. The two of them climbed into Sandy's car. "The stadium," Frank said, urgency raising the pitch of his voice.

As Sandy drove down the Coast Highway, Frank told her what had been happening. "They're going to kill Joe," he concluded, "unless we stop them." He turned on the car radio, afraid of what he might hear.

"I have to say that in all my years of watching football, I have never seen a more superbly played game," the announcer was saying. "Both teams are just magnificent."

"And it's coming down to the wire," his announcing partner commented. "Unbelievable!"

Sandy double-parked as close to a stadium entrance as she could. The three of them jumped out of the car and raced to the ticket window, then crowded through the turnstile and raced up toward the second level. A continuous roar was coming from the stadium.

"I want to get a bird's-eye view of the stadium," Frank shouted as they ran. "See if I can spot anything."

They stood in an entryway trying to catch their breath. Frank scanned the stadium. According to the scoreboard, there were six minutes to go in the game and the Toros were ahead 34–31.

Elvin Jackson was sacked for a ten-yard loss. He jumped up, slammed the ball to the ground, and raced over to House McMaran. Grabbing the lineman by the face mask, he jerked his head down to his own. Frank realized that Jackson must have seen McMaran purposely miss a block.

Incredibly, Jackson whirled the giant lineman around and sent him staggering toward the bench. And then, with fans all over the country watching, he kicked McMaran in the rear. The crowd roared.

The big lineman whirled around and rushed toward Jackson, but three of his teammates grabbed him and led him off the field.

As the Sharks' kicking team lined up to punt to the Toros, Frank scanned the players on the sideline. He spotted Number Thirteen, standing with a knot of players behind one of the coaches.

With three minutes left on the clock, the Toros wanted to eat up time. Two running plays netted five yards. They tried a screen pass on third down, but the Sharks' rushers pressured the quarterback. His pass fell incomplete.

With a minute left to play, the Sharks called time out. Frank saw Joe buckling his chin strap, preparing to take the field to receive the Toros' punt.

"That's him!" Jennifer Washington shouted. She clutched Frank's arm and pointed toward one of the photographers near the end zone, waiting for Joe to field the punt.

With a sinking heart, Frank recognized the lethal "camera" Hyde had shown him the night before. Joe would be less than twenty yards away from the man, with his back to him. The dart would catch him between his shoulder and hip pads.

Frank turned to Washington and grabbed her by the arms. "Get to Nicky Chambers's box," he shouted. "Tell him to alert security!"

Washington nodded and ran out the entryway toward an elevator that would take her to the top of the stadium.

"Let's go!" Frank shouted to Sandy. As Joe began to jog onto the field, they began their frantic race through the crowd and down the stairs toward the playing field. "Hey, watch it buddy!" someone shouted as Frank pushed past him. Out of the corner of his eye, Frank saw two ushers hurrying toward him. He could imagine what they thought, seeing his wet hair and clothes and the wild look in his eyes.

As they reached the lowest row of seats, Sandy screamed and pretended to faint, draping herself head down over the rail. As the nearest security guard rushed over to her, Frank vaulted the wall and hit the turf running.

He raced along the sidelines, shouting and waving his arms. A police officer chased after him. On the field, Joe was focused on the Toros as they broke their huddle and lined up in punt formation.

"Joe! Joe!" Frank shouted. "Run! You've got to run!"

Just before the kick sailed into the air, Joe took his eyes off the punter. His mouth dropped open in surprise when he spotted his brother on the sideline. His mouthpiece fell to the ground. "You've got to run, Joe!" Frank shouted. "Run for your life!"

Glancing into the end zone, Frank saw the photographer aiming his camera at Joe. His finger was on the trigger.

On the field Joe caught sight of the ball. Drifting back to the ten, he waited, conscious of the Toros bearing down on him, and of the late afternoon wind.

"Fair catch, Joe!" Frank heard a coach yelling.

"No!" Frank shouted. *"Run!"*

Joe did not raise his arms to signal for the fair catch. The ball settled into his hands, and he began to run. His startled teammates scrambled to set up a makeshift wall.

Joe angled to the right and turned upfield. Two would-be tacklers misjudged his speed and missed. Joe sidestepped another. At midfield he stopped on a dime and reversed direction. Now only the punter was between him and the goal line.

Joe was "in the zone." He was flying. He had no doubt he would get past the punter. His stride smooth and easy, he lulled the last Toro into believing he had the angle to make the tackle. At the twenty, the punter reached for Joe, just as he kicked into a higher gear and left the man sprawling in the grass. Running free, he crossed the goal line and gently laid the ball on the eye of the painted shark in the end zone. His teammates mobbed him.

Joyous Sharks fans were already pouring onto the field as Bobby Joe Ratliff kicked the extra point. Thousands still in the stands counted down the final seconds. Frank glanced up at the scoreboard: Sharks 38–Toros 34.

Sandy came running up, tears in her eyes and a huge grin on her face. "Can you believe it?" she shouted, wrapping her arms around Frank.

They scanned the crowd on the field, looking for Hyde's photographer. Sandy spotted him striding through a knot of fans, his eyes on the happy crush of football players surrounding Joe.

"Grab a cop," Frank said, breaking into a run. Sidestepping celebrating fans, he caught up with Hyde's man and tackled him, both of them falling to the ground. Sandy and a police officer ran up as Frank got to his knees and held the man down.

Sandy picked up the camera and handed it to the confused officer. "Careful, Officer, this is a deadly weapon," she said.

"Hold this man," Frank urged the officer. "He just tried to murder Joe Hardy."

They raced through the crowd to the elevator that took season ticket holders to their luxury sky boxes, and from there up steep, narrow stairs to the press box. The orange chopper that Frank had seen on the yacht was poised on the press box roof. Frank and Sandy burst through a door from the press box in time to see Peter Hyde and Melissa Sharpe struggling against the wind to reach the chopper.

"Mother!" Sandy shouted, and Melissa Sharpe hesitated. She turned toward her daughter. Hyde grabbed her arm, but she jerked free and ran to Sandy, sobbing.

Hyde pulled a gun and fired wildly, then opened the door to the chopper. Frank went into a cold rage. He could not bear to see the man who had planned to kill his brother get away. He raced to Hyde and grabbed him by the leg just as the chopper was lifting off the roof. Hyde, still in Frank's grasp, hung on to the door as the chopper settled clumsily back down, one skid dangling precariously over the roof's edge.

Peter Hyde looked down at the stadium parking lot far below him and took his hands off the door. Frank heard the press box door bang open behind him and turned to see two security guards rushing toward him. Fenton Hardy and Nicky Chambers were right behind them. One of them took Hyde into custody, while the other, his gun drawn, directed the pilot to get out of the chopper.

"Are you all right, son?" Fenton asked.

"I'm fine, Dad," Frank replied. "Could you believe Joe's run?" Out of the corner of his eye, Frank noticed Sandy and Melissa Sharpe, with their arms still around each other, tears in their eyes. Melissa Sharpe kissed her daughter on the cheek, then walked over to Hyde and the guard.

"You want me, too," she said quietly, and put her wrists out to be handcuffed.

The press conference in Nicky Chambers's office was packed with reporters, TV camera crews, and jubilant friends of the Sharks. Fenton Hardy stood just behind and to the left of the Sharks' owner. Chambers had presented him as the investigator who broke the case, then introduced Frank, who stood with his arm around Sandy in front of TD's aquarium.

Fenton told the crowd the background of the plot, from Bobby Walker's death to Melissa Sharpe's steroid scheme and Andrew Rosen's skimming.

"But that wasn't the main point," Frank said, taking up the story. "Hyde and his gang wanted to own the Sharks. And they were willing to do anything they had to, including committing murder."

"Will Melissa Sharpe go to jail?" a reporter asked.

Chambers glanced in Sandy's direction, a distressed look on his face. "I suspect so," he said, "as will Andrew Rosen, though I must say in Rosen's favor that he has shown remorse. He has offered to pay back what he stole and will testify against Hyde."

"What about House McMaran?" another reporter asked.

"My chief of security tells me he's in custody," Chambers replied. "He'll be banned from professional football. Although I'm no lawyer, I suspect he and several other Sharks will spend time in prison. So will our head trainer, Jennifer Washington, although I will be happy to recommend leniency because of the invaluable assistance she provided today."

"So does Nicky Chambers hold on to his team?" a voice in the crowd asked.

"Nicky Chambers will never sell the Sharks, for any price," the owner replied, smiling. He peered at the crowd. "But enough of these questions," he shouted into the microphone. "We've got a division championship to celebrate!"

A cheer went up as Elvin Jackson and Rich Havranek, still in uniform, were ushered into the room.

Then Joe Hardy walked in, also still in uniform. He gave big hugs to his father, Frank, and Sandy, then shook hands with Nicky Chambers, who threw his arms around the Sharks' newest hero. The cheering would not stop.

A reporter waved his hand and shouted, "Nicky, I've got a question for Joe Hardy. Joe, we just got word you were voted the game's most valuable player. So what next for the Sharks' hottest rookie?"

Joe grinned. "I'm glad you asked that question. I have an announcement to make. Effective this afternoon, I am retiring and returning to my hometown of Bayport. My break's almost over, and I can't afford to miss a day of school."

Frank and Joe's next case:

Frank and Joe make a special trip to the Bayport Fairgrounds to check out the steeplechase races. They want to catch the champion horse Against All Odds in action. Fast, fit, and powerful, he's a stallion with a million-dollar future ahead of him. But suddenly all bets are off. Soon after the race, the boys discover that Against All Odds has disappeared. The Hardys know this is more than a simple case of horse thievery. Whoever took the champion is a master of deception, diversion, and intimidation. And the stakes in the race to recover the horse couldn't be higher. Frank and Joe are in hot pursuit of a ruthless and desperate criminal—one willing to kill to cover his tracks . . . in *Against All Odds,* Case #96 in The Hardy Boys Casefiles™.